CLOSE YOUR EYES

THOMAS FINCHAM

Close Your Eyes
Thomas Fincham

Copyright © 2017
All Rights Reserved.

AUTHOR'S NOTE
This book is a work of fiction. Names, characters, places and incidents are products of the author's imagination or are used fictitiously. Any resemblance to actual events or locales or persons, living or dead, is entirely coincidental.

The scanning, uploading and distribution of this book via the internet or any other means without the permission of the publisher is illegal and punishable by law. Please purchase only authorized electronic editions, and do not participate in or encourage electronic piracy of copyrighted materials. Your support of the author's rights is appreciated.

Visit the author's website:
www.finchambooks.com

Contact:
finchambooks@gmail.com

Join my Facebook page:
https://www.facebook.com/finchambooks/

MARTIN RHODES

1) Close Your Eyes
2) Cross Your Heart
3) Say Your Prayers
4) Fear Your Enemy

ONE

Tammy Lynn McGuire rocked slightly as the subway train moved at a swift pace. She wore a purple sweatshirt, gray sweatpants, pink runners, and her hair was pulled back in a ponytail.

She was staring at her finger. A white line marked where she once wore her wedding ring. Her eyes welled up with tears, but she controlled herself. There were passengers sitting around her, and she did not want to cause a scene.

She had never suspected her marriage was doomed. *Maybe that's how it always is*, she thought.

Her husband, Rick, had moved out of their two-bedroom apartment and was now living with his mistress. He did not even give her a chance to kick him out. He just came home one day and said he was leaving.

She couldn't believe it had come to this. Rick had been her high school sweetheart. They had married right after they had graduated. It was a small wedding, for sure. No church. No fancy reception. No expensive honeymoon.

They got married in Rick's uncle's backyard. They had erected a tent where guests could sit. There were not that many, to begin with. They found an ordained minister online to officiate at the wedding. Afterward, all the guests were invited to an all-you-can-eat Chinese buffet. Their honeymoon was a long drive to Las Vegas, which her mom paid for. Tammy did not care for a dream wedding. She was just happy to have the man of her dreams.

She shook her head whenever she thought of Rick. She was only eighteen when she decided to tie the knot with him. What did she know about men and marriage then?

After her honeymoon, she wanted to go to college and become a nurse. Instead, she took a job as a waitress to help pay for Rick to get his auto mechanic license. Rick eventually landed a job for a big company that owned several garages. When her time came to apply to colleges, she became pregnant with their son, Rick Junior.

The boy was now five years old. He was the most beautiful thing in her life.

Her son sat next to her, entertaining himself by bouncing a ball. On a few occasions, she had to tell him not to bounce the ball too hard. "There are passengers getting on and off the train at each stop, Rick. You could hit someone with that."

Right after Rick Jr. was born, she decided to stay home and take care of him. After all, being a waitress did not pay her enough to afford daycare. She hoped that once Rick Jr. was old enough to go to kindergarten, she would follow her dream and enroll in college.

Over the years, she had visited many colleges and had picked up brochures and information pamphlets. She had even checked out online seminars on the steps to becoming a nurse.

During this time, Rick was very supportive of her. He assured her that he would help pay for her dream, like she had helped pay for his. Rick loved being a mechanic, and he always told her that, one day, he would have his own garage.

She believed him because she loved him.

She also believed that he would take care of her.

What she did not know was that for the past six months, he had been having an affair with the secretary at his garage. She was younger than Tammy Lynn, but according to Rick, she had her own place and no wild dreams she kept nagging him about.

Tammy Lynn did not understand why he would think her wanting to become a nurse was nagging. She thought, *If I got a good job, wouldn't that help us financially?*

Regardless, when their marriage ended, she could not get a job that would pay enough to support her and her son. She had been out of the workforce for over five years, and with no post-secondary education on her résumé, there were not many jobs open to her. Rick had left her with just enough money to pay for food and one month's rent.

Seeing no other option, she turned to her mother.

With her mother's help, Tammy got a job at the same bottling factory where her mom worked. It was hard work with long hours, but what choice did she have? Fortunately, the supervisor was nice and understanding. He alternated shifts between her and her mother. This allowed one of them to look after Rick Jr. while the other went to work.

Tammy spotted a man sitting across from her. The train moved from side to side, but the man's body remained erect. She realized that all through the ride, the man had not once moved. He was wearing a beige trench coat. His eyes were covered by sunglasses, and it looked like his hands were pulled inside his sleeves.

Maybe he is asleep, she thought.

She watched as the train stopped at a station and more people got on and off.

The train moved again, and Rick Jr.'s ball slipped out of his hands. It rolled across the floor and hit the man's shoes.

Rick Jr. looked over at his mother. He was too afraid to go and pick it up.

"I warned you not to bounce the ball too hard," Tammy Lynn said, scolding him.

"Sorry, mommy," he replied.

She smiled and patted him on the head. She could never be angry with him. He was the one bright light in her world right now.

She leaned over to the man. "Excuse me, do you mind kicking the ball over, please?"

The man did not stir.

She tried again, this time a little louder. "Can you kick over my son's ball?"

No response.

She shook her head. *Some people are not one bit courteous.*

She got up and stormed over to him.

When she leaned down to pick up the ball, she froze.

The man had not pulled his hands inside his jacket sleeves. They were completely missing as if someone had cut them off.

Shocked, she looked up at the man. His skin was pale and his lips had started to turn blue.

Horrified, she turned and ran over to Rick Jr. She grabbed him and pulled the emergency brake lever.

The train squealed to a halt as the emergency brakes took hold. The noise was loud and deafening, more than enough to mask her screams.

TWO

The office was small, but the walls were decorated with certificates and other designations. Dr. Jacob Cohen was a lead medical specialist at Bridgeton Mercy Hospital. He had graduated at the top of his class from Harvard Medical School. After several years at Massachusetts General Hospital, Dr. Cohen decided to move to the city of Bridgeton.

The woman glanced at her watch but did not complain. She had been to Dr. Cohen's office many times. Dr. Cohen was a specialist, but he always made room in his busy schedule for her.

She could see the Bridgeton Harbor from the window. She wished she was there right now. In fact, she wished she was anywhere but here.

She adjusted her leather jacket and her hip holster.

Special Agent Johanna Pullinger of the Federal Bureau of Investigation was not known for being patient or sitting idle. Jo, as she was known, was an energetic go-getter with a type-A personality.

She was five-ten with short blonde hair and striking green eyes, and she was in great shape except for one thing: she had been getting chest pains again. She had a rare heart condition, which had first been diagnosed when she was a baby. Doctors predicted she would not live past her fifth birthday. Miraculously, she did. They then predicted that she would not be active in sports and other physical activities. She proved them wrong by becoming the best basketball player in the state. To top it off, she ran several marathons, including the Boston Marathon and the New York Marathon.

When she applied to the bureau, her doctor at the time advised her against applying. She would not pass the physical, he said. Her heart would not take the stress.

She turned to Dr. Cohen. He was a family friend. But more importantly, he was her father's friend. He agreed to be her doctor but under one condition: if her health worsened for any reason, she should come to him immediately.

The door swung open, and Dr. Cohen entered. "Sorry for the delay," he said. "We had an emergency."

He sat behind his desk. He was short, bald, had a grayish beard, and his glasses were perched on his thin nose.

"When did the pain start?" he asked, skipping the pleasantries.

"This morning, when I was going up the stairs in my house," she replied.

"Describe the pain."

"It was sharp and strong. It felt like my entire chest would cave in."

He nodded. "Hmm…"

He pulled off his glasses, leaned back in his chair and stared at her.

His gaze burned into her. She knew what he was about to say next.

"Have you reconsidered what we had discussed before?" he asked.

"I'm not ready for a heart transplant," she said.

"Let me at least put you on the waiting list. It can be more than six months before we even find the right donor. Plus, with your rare blood type, it may take even longer. That should give you enough time to think this over."

She shook her head. "No."

"Jo," he said gently. "Right now, your condition is not life-threatening. But the way things are going, your health could deteriorate unexpectedly. I would rather be ready if and when that happened."

"No," she said.

"As your doctor and a medical professional, I advise you to reconsider."

"I can't be away from my job for too long."

"If you keep pushing yourself the way you are now, you might not have a job. And, if the operation is successful, you could be back to work in a year or even six months."

"It's still too long."

He sighed. "You're stubborn, just like your father, you know that. I couldn't get through to him when he was alive. I doubt I can get through to you now." He put on his glasses and glanced at her file. "How is the pain now?"

"It's gone."

"Gone as in its-no-longer-there or gone as in I-don't-want-my-doctor-to-know?"

"It's gone. I don't feel it anymore."

"Okay, that's good to hear. I'll write you a prescription." He scribbled something on a pad. "The medication may not be as effective, but take them anyway. They won't replace a transplant, but they'll help somewhat."

He tore off the sheet and slid it across his desk.

She grabbed the note, and without looking, she stuffed it in her jacket pocket.

Her cell phone rang. She checked the number. "It's work. I have to go."

Dr. Cohen stood up and came around the desk. He put his hand on her shoulder. "Anything happens, you give me a call, okay?"

She nodded and smiled. "I will."

THREE

The truck pulled into the gas station and stopped at a pump.

A man got out of the passenger's side. He was six-foot-four with salt and pepper hair and deep blue eyes. He was also clean-shaven. He had on a black coat, which hung loosely on his broad shoulders. In his hand was a duffel bag. The bag contained all his belongings: one shirt, one pair of jeans, a couple of socks, and some underwear. There was also a ziplock bag of toiletries, but nothing more.

He examined his surroundings.

Next to the gas station was a diner. He had not eaten since he hitched a ride. The truck driver was sixty-two years old, and he delivered produce between states. During the trip, he had offered his passenger some sandwiches, but he politely declined. The driver was already giving him a free ride. He did not feel comfortable having his lunch given to him free as well.

The man waved goodbye to the driver, who was busy fueling the truck. The driver had another six-hour journey ahead of him. He had been kind enough to take a detour to drop his passenger off, so he was in a hurry to get back on the road.

The driver waved back with a smile.

The man entered the diner and headed straight for the bathroom. He went to the sink and filled his hands with cold water. He splashed his face and then stared at his image in the mirror.

Martin Rhodes could not believe he was living the life of a vagabond. He had no money and no home. He was once a respected homicide detective for the Newport Police Department, but one single action had turned his life upside down.

He had gone from catching criminals to becoming one. He had spent ten years in prison for murder. It was initially life, but when new evidence emerged, his sentence was cut to fifteen years. This was further shortened when he was given parole due to good behavior.

Rhodes had been picked up from the Newport Transfer Facility by Hyder Ali, a reporter for the *Daily Times*, a newspaper in the city of Franklin. Ali was friends with Detective Tom Nolan. Nolan was the one who had discovered the evidence that ultimately allowed Rhodes to walk free. Had Nolan not pursued the case, Rhodes would have still been rotting in prison.

Rhodes's stay in Franklin was not uneventful. He had helped Ali catch the Franklin Strangler, a serial killer who was targeting random citizens.

Rhodes quickly realized his time in Franklin was coming to an end when Ali requested an exclusive interview. Rhodes was, after all, a former detective who had served time for murder. Rhodes agreed to the interview, but under two conditions: Ali did not ask any questions about the night of the murder, and that Ali printed the interview once Rhodes had left Franklin.

Rhodes had no desire for any further attention. He had had his share of the spotlight during his trial, and the last thing he wanted was the media hounding him now that he was out of prison.

After leaving Franklin, Rhodes wandered from town to town, looking for work. One opportune call to Nolan led him to a town called Parish. His ex-wife needed his help to exonerate her current husband, who had been charged with murder. Rhodes was nearly broke when he had arrived in Parish. Fortunately, at the end of his stay, some money came his way. He never asked for the money, but it was given to him as a token of appreciation.

Rhodes thought the money would last a good while, and it would have, had it not been for a woman.

He frowned. *It is always a woman.*

He should have been suspicious the moment she told him her name. *Daisy.*

He was staying at a run-down motel in the town of Salem. Daisy was in the room next to his. He spotted her a few times, and one day, they spoke to each other.

She told him she was running away from an abusive boyfriend. Rhodes felt sorry for her. She was young and pretty, and she told him she came from a small town in the west.

He took her out to a fast-food restaurant. He made a big mistake when he pulled out an envelope, which held all his money and paid for the meal.

The dinner was pleasant. They talked, and he kind of liked her. She laughed at all his jokes, which should have been a red flag. Rhodes was never known for his humor. But having spent ten years behind bars, he was excited that a girl was giving him attention.

After their meal, they took a walk around town. She put her arm around his as they did. He didn't stop her. After what she had told him about her boyfriend, he wanted to protect her. Plus, it was nice to have a woman want his company.

Moving from town to town had left him feeling lonely. Rhodes was once married, but when he was sentenced for murder, the marriage swiftly fell apart. The dissolution of the marriage was his fault, and Rhodes was grateful that he had been able to make amends with his ex-wife in Parish.

When he and Daisy reached their motel, she offered him a drink in her room. She had picked up some liquor from the previous motel she had stayed at.

Stupidly, Rhodes agreed.

He shook his head whenever he thought about what happened next.

A few drinks later, Rhodes passed out on the bed. When he woke up, he was still clothed, but Daisy was not in her room. In fact, when he looked around, he saw that even her stuff was gone.

Rhodes checked his coat. The envelope with all his money was not there.

He rushed to his room and found the door open.

Inside, his duffel bag and all his belongings were scattered on his bed.

Daisy had taken the cash, but she left his stuff behind. There wasn't anything valuable, to begin with. Plus, she could now buy whatever she wanted with the money she stole from him.

Rhodes splashed his face with more cold water.

He kicked himself for being so naïve. He couldn't really blame himself, though. He had spent too many days and nights inside a six-by-eight cell, which had dulled his instincts. The world was a cruel place and didn't follow the same rules he had followed during his time in prison.

Whatever happened in prison stayed in prison.

If you got messed with by an inmate, you dealt with that inmate the next time you saw him.

Rhodes was certain he would never see Daisy again.

He dried his face and left the washroom.

He went up to the counter and dropped some change on it. The waitress looked at the change and then brought him a cup of coffee and a bagel.

"I'm afraid that's all you can get with what you have," she said to Rhodes.

"It'll do," he replied.

He took a bite of the bagel and then grabbed a newspaper lying on the seat next to him.

Bridgeton was a big city, and he wanted to know everything about it now that he was here.

FOUR

Jo arrived at the Dupont Subway Station.

The area had already been secured by the FBI. Yellow police tape surrounded the station entrance. A large group of passengers was lining up to board shuttle buses sent by the Bridgeton Transit Authority.

Jo already knew that a dead body had been found on the train, which meant all travel between stations had been halted.

Jo flashed her credentials to the agent at the entrance and proceeded down a flight of stairs. The tunnel leading to the train platform was eerily empty. Normally, there would be dozens of passengers moving in and out of the tunnel, but not today.

She went down another flight of stairs and, after flashing her credentials once again, was allowed to pass through the ticket booth.

She was greeted by Special Agent in Charge Charlotte Walters. Walters had cropped gray hair, and her face was etched with deep wrinkles. She used to be a heavy smoker but had quit a few years back. Her gray eyes were devoid of excitement, but Jo knew her mind was always racing in order to be a step ahead of the perpetrators.

"What've we got?" Jo asked.

"A passenger on the 10:20 train discovered the body. She said it was already there when she got on."

"What station?" Jo asked.

"What?"

"At what station did she get on?"

"I think she said Chester Station."

Jo did a quick calculation in her head. "That's nine stations before she discovered it. Where is she now?"

Walters nodded towards the end of the platform. A woman and a boy were standing next to a paramedic. Jo could tell the woman was clearly shaken up.

A man appeared on the platform.

"We've got trouble," Walters said.

The man stormed up to them. Chief Vincent Baker of the Bridgeton Police Department was tall, imposing, and he had a large gut that was barely held in by his police uniform. He was known for his loud, unexpected outbursts.

"This is not your crime scene," he growled.

"Good morning to you too, Chief Baker," Walters replied calmly.

"We can handle this," Baker said. "We don't need the FBI."

"I'm sure you can," Walters said. "But we got the call."

Baker frowned. "What?"

"Someone called into our command center and informed us that there would be a dead body on the train."

"Then why didn't you tell us?"

"We didn't have time," Walters replied.

He stared at her.

"We received the tip around the same time the call came in from the Transit Authority."

Baker's eyes glinted with skepticism.

Walters crossed her arms over her chest. "Okay, if you want to take over, I'll have my team removed immediately. It'll be your case, but you better bring your guys in fast. BTA wants us to move the body as soon as possible. They can't hold the train on the platform for long. It's causing a service disruption. I'm sure you saw the large group of passengers outside."

Baker understood he was between a rock and a hard place. He hated having to yield to the FBI, but he also didn't have the resources to quickly move in and take over.

"Fine," he said. "But you keep us informed of what you find."

"Don't we always," Walters replied without smiling.

FIVE

Outside the Dupont station, a van pulled up by the curb. The decal across the side of the van read *BN-24*. BN-24 was the number one news channel in the city. It used to be called the Bridgeton Television Network, but when management decided to create a 24-hour news station, BN-24 was born.

BN-24 had started off covering mostly entertainment stories. Dog and cat shows, Easter and Christmas parades, and food and music festivals. But now it was turning to more hard-hitting news: crime, corruption, and murder.

Their star reporter on these stories was Ellen Sheehan. Ellen was in the passenger seat of the news van. The driver's name was Walt Felton, and he was also the cameraman.

Ellen looked around the scene. "Do you see any other news vans?" she asked.

"I don't think so," Walt replied. Walt wore a checkered shirt, jeans, and boots. He also had a goatee, and his baseball cap was pulled on backward.

"Look carefully," Ellen ordered him. She pulled down the visor, checked her face in the mirror, and reapplied makeup to her face. Her hair was red, her eyes were green, and she had freckles on her cheeks. She wore a dark red suit, white pearls around her neck, and red lipstick.

"I think I see someone," Walt said. His head was sticking out the window.

"Who?" she yelled.

"I think it's the Sun." SUNTV was the second most-watched news channel in the city. They were always focused on the so-called serious stories, but lately, they had seen their viewership move over to their rival, BN-24.

"I hope it's not that slut Janie," Ellen spat.

Janie Fernandez was tall, dark, and beautiful. She was also once Miss New Mexico. Janie had dabbled in modeling but decided that she wanted to devote herself to more important issues in life. Janie had covered topics ranging from illegal immigrants to environmental disasters to stock market fraud.

Janie was everything Ellen was not: respected and highly intelligent.

"Let's go. They're getting out," Ellen said.

Ellen dashed in her heels and secured a spot in front of the entrance to the station. "Hurry up," she said to Walt, who was adjusting his camera.

Janie walked over to her.

"We were here first," Ellen said.

Janie smiled. "That's fine. There's room for everyone."

"I don't think there is enough room for your big ego," Ellen replied.

"I could say the same to you."

SUNTV's cameraman, Jeff Lodgson, came over and bumped fists with Walt. Jeff was dressed in a T-shirt, cargo pants, and his baseball cap was pulled on backward as well. Unlike their bosses, Walt and Jeff had no animosity for one another. In fact, the two would go out for drinks whenever they got the chance.

Janie said, "Shouldn't you be at some bakeshop to find out who had baked the biggest cake in Bridgeton?"

"Shouldn't you be at some bikini contest to find out who can count to ten and knows the complete alphabet?" Ellen snapped back.

Janie curled her lips and stormed away.

Ellen couldn't help but smile. She turned to Walt and said, "Are you ready?"

He turned on the camera.

"Make sure you get a good shot of me, got it?"

"Sure," he said, and he pressed the record button.

SIX

Jo left Walters and Baker and moved down the train platform. She knew which car the body was in. The entire length of the compartment was surrounded by yellow tape.

She spotted an open train door and ducked underneath the tape. In the middle of the compartment, a man wearing white overalls was leaning over the victim.

The man in the overalls looked up and smiled. Ben Nakamura was the bureau's medical examiner. He was short, chubby, and known for wearing colorful T-shirts and watches. He also wore prescription glasses. But what made him stand out from the crowd was that somehow Ben always found a way to color-coordinate all his accessories. One day Jo saw him wear an orange T-shirt, orange trousers, an orange watch, orange sneakers, and even orange glasses. When she told him he looked like a fruit, he smiled and said there was more. He pulled up his pants and revealed his orange socks. Even his cell phone case was orange. Today, however, he was wearing overalls, but Jo noted his navy blue glasses. She was certain everything underneath his outer attire was the same color as well.

He looked at Jo and said, "When I saw Chief Baker, I thought I was going to be kicked out."

"We're still in charge." She glanced over at the victim. The victim was wearing a beige trench coat, black pants, white shoes, and his sunglasses were next to him in a plastic bag. Ben had already tagged the glasses.

"Find anything worth telling me?"

"The victim is male, Caucasian, between forty to forty-five years of age, weighing approximately a hundred and eighty pounds. Oh, and the victim's hands are missing." Ben pointed at the stumps.

Jo leaned down. "Were they removed before or after he was killed?"

"If I had to make an educated guess, I would say before. But I could be wrong once I put him on my table and discover something else."

"It looks like it was done with a crude instrument," Jo said, squinting. "Maybe a hacksaw?"

"Possibly."

"Do we know who he is?"

Ben shook his head. "I found no ID on him and I've got no hands to take fingerprints from. I'll have to do a DNA analysis once I get back to the lab."

"Time of death?" Jo asked.

"I would have to say ten to fourteen hours."

"This means he was murdered sometime last night and then brought here in the morning. How did the killer leave the body on the train without anyone noticing it?"

Ben put his hands up. "That's your job to find out. I just tell you how they died, not who killed them."

Jo pulled out her cell phone and snapped photos of the body from different angles.

"I've got something for you," Ben said.

She turned to him.

He walked over to his bag and pulled out a paperback. "I found it at a flea market. I think you'll find it interesting."

"And why is that?"

"It examines all the unsolved serial killings in the United States."

"Okay, but why are you giving it to me?"

"There is a chapter on the Bridgeton Ripper."

Jo snatched the book from him. "How did I miss this in my research?" she said, flipping through the pages.

"It was written twenty years ago. The publisher was a small-time press. I don't think it's even in print anymore."

She found the chapter and looked up at him. "This is a great find."

He grinned. "I thought so too."

Jo had spent a major part of her adult life trying to find out who the Bridgeton Ripper was. Even though the killings occurred over twenty years ago, they had affected her on a personal level.

Jo had read up on everything about the case. She wanted to leave no stone unturned. If there was any information out there that could help her solve the mystery, Jo wanted her hands on it.

When Ben found out her obsession, he offered to help her. He was a self-proclaimed geek, and his specialty was death. It fascinated him to the point that he made conducting forensic examinations on human cadavers his profession.

She stuffed the paperback in her jacket pocket. "Thanks, Ben. I really appreciate this."

He smiled. "No problemo."

"I'm done. You can move the body. Let me know what you find."

"Will do."

Jo flipped through the photos on her phone. She was about to exit the train when she stopped. She enlarged the image on the screen and then quickly turned back.

"Hold on," she said.

Ben had already pulled off his latex gloves. "What is it?"

"I think I saw something underneath the trench coat. Give me your gloves."

Ben handed them to her. "What did you see?" he asked, eagerly.

She pulled the gloves on and said, "It doesn't look like he is wearing a shirt underneath the coat."

"So? Why is that important?"

"The weather is cool outside. You wouldn't leave your home with nothing on underneath."

She slowly unbuttoned the coat and pulled it open.

Ben's mouth dropped.

Carved into the victim's chest were the words *WHAT THE HANDS TOUCH*. They looked like they had been etched using a chisel.

SEVEN

Jo came out of the train and found Walters standing by the platform wall. "Anything?" she asked, looking up from her phone.

"The killer left a message for us," Jo replied.

"Where?"

"On his body."

Walters's steely gaze masked her inner thoughts. She had seen enough weird events in her career that nothing surprised her anymore.

Jo said, "Ben will remove the body for further examination."

Walters nodded and then pointed toward the end of the platform. "Do you want to speak to the woman who found the body? We already have her statement. I can let her go."

Jo thought for a moment. "Give me two minutes."

She walked over to the bench where Tammy Lynn and Rick Jr. sat. Jo was already briefed on their names, and as she approached, she could tell they were anxious to leave. *It must have been shocking to find a dead person while on your way to work*, she thought.

"I'm Special Agent Jo Pullinger," Jo said. "How are you holding up?"

The woman had her arm around her son. "We're fine. How is he? I mean... he's dead, right?"

"Yes."

"What happened to his hands?" Tammy Lynn asked.

"We don't know, but we're trying to find out. Did you notice anyone sitting next to him?"

"I guess so. There were people coming in and out of the train all the time. If there's even one empty seat, you take it, or else you'll be standing for your entire ride."

"Was he alone when you boarded the train at Chester Station?"

She looked down at her shoes, rallying her thoughts. "I don't think so."

"Who was also there?"

"An old lady. I remember her because she smiled at Rick Jr. But she got off a few stations later."

Jo frowned. If the old lady was already there, this meant whoever left the body was already gone.

"Didn't you find it odd that the man never once moved during your train ride?" Jo asked. Tammy Lynn shrugged. "In the morning you see people sleeping all the time. I nap on the train after I've completed my night shift at the factory. I honestly had no idea there was something wrong with him." She then squeezed the boy. "I'm just worried for my son. My husband and I are going through a separation, and now, you know, he had to see this."

The boy had his head held low. He was focused on bouncing a ball.

Jo got down on her knees and said, "How are you doing?"

"Good. I guess," he replied, not looking up at her.

"What did you see on the train?"
"The man."
"What happened to the man?"
"He's dead."
"Does that make you scared?"

He shrugged. "I don't know."

"I don't think you're scared," Jo said.

He looked up at her.

"I think you are very brave, you know that?"

His eyes widened in surprise. "I am?"

"Sure. I talked to people and they said you were not scared. You made sure to hold your mom's hand, and you took care of her." It was a white lie. Jo had not spoken to any of the passengers yet, but she did not want what happened tonight to affect the boy in any way. She had a niece of her own, and she would never want her to see what this boy had.

Rick Jr. smiled at her.

"You're free to go," Jo said.

She watched as the mother and son left the platform, holding each other's hand as they walked.

Jo spotted a man in a transit uniform standing by the front of the train. She went up to him.

"Are you the supervisor?" she asked.

He nodded. "Dennis Wilmont."

"Special Agent Pullinger." Jo showed Wilmont her credentials. "So, what happened here?"

"When the lady pulled the emergency lever, the engineer immediately stopped the train."

"Where is the engineer?" Jo asked.

The supervisor waved over another man. He was also dressed in a transit uniform. "This is Mike Schwartz. Mike, tell the agent what you did."

The engineer cleared his throat. "The moment the alarm went off, I was in the tunnel between stations. The trains are equipped with automatic brakes in case of an emergency. I was able to slow the train down manually. Per protocol, I quickly walked the length of the train, going from car to car until I found the body. I didn't touch it, but I could tell he was not alive. I quickly informed Dennis, and he instructed me to pull into the next station."

The supervisor spoke up. "When the train pulled up, we already had our officers waiting for it at the platform." BTA also had security officers. They were trained by the Bridgeton Police but they did not carry a firearm. But they did have the authority to detain unruly passengers until the police arrived. "We emptied the train and closed off all exit and entry to the station. The passengers from the train have been detained until you guys tell us what to do."

Jo had seen a large group of people on the main floor of the station. "Get their names and contact info, and let them go. I doubt the killer stuck around for us to show up."

The supervisor nodded.

"Do you have cameras inside the train?" she asked.

The supervisor shook his head. "Only on the platforms and the entrances and exits to the stations."

"Can I see the footage?"

EIGHT

Ellen stopped a transit employee by thrusting her microphone in his face. "Ellen Sheehan from BN-24. Can you tell us who the victim is?"

The officer looked like a deer caught in the headlights. "Um... I'm not sure. The FBI is on the scene."

"Do you know who's in charge? Can you bring them to us for an interview?"

"Um... I have to go," he said and rushed away.

Ellen looked over at Janie. She was also interviewing a transit employee. The employee was more than willing to speak to her. Janie had her hand on his elbow, and whenever she asked him a question, he answered her with a smile. It also helped that she was smiling too and was paying attention to his every word.

Ellen seethed. Janie was a natural at getting interviews, but Ellen had to work at it.

She had spent years covering frivolous stories, and when BN-24 was created, she jumped at the opportunity. There were only so many magic weight loss programs she could cover before she lost her mind.

Ellen took care of how she looked, which meant she was careful with what she put in her body. She could not stand people who thought they could be skinny by taking a pill when they were still eating a large slice of chocolate cake each night.

One woman swore that all she did was drink a glass of her weight loss powder, and for the rest of the day, she indulged to her heart's delight. Ellen was so tempted to tell her off on the air by revealing she had seen the woman regularly working out at her local gym. And there was no way in hell the woman was drinking the green junk she was selling because in between workouts, the woman only drank water.

Ellen felt that by interviewing such charlatans, she was complicit in selling their lies to the public. However, if she got a cut of the sales, then that was a different matter. And if people were so gullible and naïve to think that, without any sacrifice, they could look like a supermodel on TV, they deserved to have their money taken from them.

A group of people emerged from the station entrance. Ellen grabbed a man with multiple piercings and said, "Ellen Sheehan from BN-24. Can you tell us what you saw inside? Did you see the victim?"

The man shook his head. "I was at the front of the train, but I heard someone say the man walked in by himself and then collapsed on the seat."

"So, are you saying he was not murdered?"

The pierced man looked confused.

"Then why is the FBI involved?" Ellen added.

He shrugged. "Maybe he was shot and then he collapsed on the seat."

Ellen pushed him aside and thrust the microphone in front of another person. He was dressed in a suit and looked annoyed. "They wouldn't let us go, like we were guilty of something," he said.

"What did the FBI ask you?" Ellen said, seeing her chance for an interview.

"I have to go. I'm already late for work. My boss is going to kill me."

The man pushed by her.

Ellen looked over at Janie. She and the cameraman were already packing up. Janie had gotten her story. Ellen had nothing.

Walt asked, "You want me to get a long shot of the scene?"

"Sure, why not."

An old woman approached Ellen. She turned to her, her eyes gleaming with annoyance. "Can I help you?"

"Are you Ellen Sheehan from BN-24?" the woman asked.

"I am."

The woman smiled. "I'm a big fan of yours. I watch you on TV every day."

Ellen sighed. "Thank you."

"I was on the train with the dead man," the woman added.

Ellen's eyes lit up. She nodded to Walt. He turned the camera on the woman. "This is Ellen Sheehan from BN-24. Can you describe what you saw on the train?"

"Yes, I can," the woman replied. "I was sitting near the man but I didn't know he was dead. It was only when a woman screamed that I knew something was wrong. I turned and saw the man had his chin resting on his chest."

"What did he look like?"

"He was white, and he had on a long coat, but I will tell you something you won't believe."

"What?" Ellen eagerly asked.

"The man's hands were missing."

Ellen paused a moment. "Are you saying the man's hands were cut off?"

"That's exactly what I'm saying."

Not another nut job, Ellen thought.

The woman said, "That's what made the other woman scream. She was staring at his missing hands."

Ellen's eyes narrowed. "And you are certain you saw he had no hands?"

The woman's eyes narrowed. "Yes, of course, I did. If I didn't, I wouldn't say it. I'm not crazy, you know."

"Of course not," Ellen said. "I just need to make sure for the viewers." She gave the woman a reassuring smile and asked her a few more questions.

After the interview, Ellen turned to Walt. "When the FBI holds their news conference, I'm going to confirm what the woman just told us. Make sure you get a shot of me asking this question, got it?"

"Sure," Walt said. *That's what I always do*, he wanted to add but held his tongue. They recorded segments for the lead-up to the evening news. Ellen then stormed back to the news van.

NINE

The transit security office was located on the main platform of the station behind a two-way mirror.

An attractive woman came up to the window and began fixing her makeup.

The transit officers on duty gave each other a high five. "Best seats in the house," one of them quipped.

Jo did not find their antics amusing. In many ways, they were indulging in voyeurism, watching unsuspecting people go about their daily lives. But she knew there was no other way to monitor what was going on at each station.

Safety was vital. Without security, people would be hesitant to take public transit. The Bridgeton Transit Authority was once a haven for crime. Drugs were easily transferred from passenger to passenger. Pickpockets moved from station to station. Criminals used the subway as their mode of escape. And to top it off, there were frequent instances of suicidal people coming to a station just to jump in front of an arriving train. The jumpers became so bad that BTA implemented a policy where no incident of suicide would be passed on to the media. They feared if people saw how common the problem was, they would be encouraged to jump as well.

With the gag order in place, the jumpers went from four or five a week to one a week.

The transit officers, along with regular employees, were trained to spot any signs of a would-be jumper. But more often than not, they were too late to stop suicide.

Jo and Supervisor Wilmont turned their attention to a row of computer monitors. Each screen showed the station from a different angle. "Our security offices in each station are all linked," Wilmont said.

Jo said, "Tammy Lynn McGuirre and her son got on at Chester Station. They confirmed the victim was already there when they sat down. This means he had to have been dropped off by someone at an earlier station. How long is the ride between stations?"

"The trains run every two to three minutes during rush hour," Wilmont said. "But outside of rush hour, it's more like four to five minutes."

Jo thought about it. "If its non-rush hour, can you find out what time the train departed from its first stop?"

"That's easy," Wilmont replied. He picked up a clipboard and scanned it. He flipped one page and then another. "It was Mike Schwartz's shift, so Train 407 started its journey at Wellington Station."

"Can you pull up the video for that train?" Jo asked Wilmont.

"Sure."

The officer began typing on the keyboard. A few seconds later, he pointed at a screen.

The camera was aimed at the subway platform. The sign on the station wall read *Wellington.* It was the first station on the east to west line. The clock on the screen told her it was thirty-five minutes before the body was discovered.

"Mike's pulling into the station now," the supervisor said.

The train arrived and came to a halt. The train doors opened, and passengers began getting on and off.

"Can you pause that?" Jo said.

The image froze.

She looked closely, but none of the passengers fit the description of the victim.

"Okay, run it."

The doors opened and the passengers got on. The train left the station.

"Can we follow it?" Jo asked.

The officer at the keyboard said, "We can get a visual on it at the next station."

The officer brought up the relevant footage of Train #407. Again, Jo examined the passengers waiting for the train, and again, she did not see the victim.

The video moved from station to station. More passengers got on and got off.

At one of the stations, a connecting one, a large group had gathered on the platform. Jo and the transit officers had to go through each angle of the platform to see if anyone matching the victim's description entered. After reviewing the footage several times, they moved on.

Jo was beginning to get the feeling they might have missed something. There was no other way for the victim to end up on the train without boarding at a station.

When the train had left the yard, Schwartz had checked each compartment, and he confirmed the train was empty when he began his journey. If the train was not, he would have raised the alarm.

No. The killer did not want the body to be found by a transit officer. BTA and the local police would have hidden the gruesome find from the public.

The killer had chopped off the victim's hands and carved a message on his chest. And the way the body was disguised as a regular passenger indicated the killer wanted an audience. *The killer wanted the citizens of Bridgeton to know what he had done.*

The footage had moved on to other stations by the time Jo pointed at the monitor and shouted, "There!"

The victim was clearly visible thanks to his trench coat. He was accompanied by another man who was wearing a jacket, a hoodie, and a baseball cap.

He is shielding his identity, Jo thought.

The two walked up to the edge of the platform.

Jo narrowed her eyes. There was something odd about the way they walked. The left step of the man and right step of the victim were in unison as if their legs were held together.

When Jo looked closely, she could see the man's arm was around the victim's waist.

He carried him aboard!

The train pulled up, the doors opened, and the suspect and the victim boarded.

"What station is that?" Jo asked.

"Davenport," Wilmont replied.

The train exited the terminal, and the footage flipped to the next station: Broadview.

When the doors opened, the man in the baseball cap got off and disappeared from view. The image flipped to another angle of the station. They watched as the man came up the stairs and then exited through the ticket booth.

No one paid any attention to him. *And why would they?* Jo thought. *He was just another person using public transit.*

"Do you have cameras outside?" Jo asked.

The supervisor shook his head. "We don't."

Jo gritted her teeth. She had just watched the killer walk away.

TEN

Rhodes spent the afternoon walking the streets of Bridgeton. He wanted to absorb the sights and sounds of the city.

During his time in prison, he had read a lot of books. One of the books talked about places to settle down if someone decided to immigrate to the U.S.A. But Rhodes was not an immigrant. He was born and raised in America, but he had been locked away from society for ten years. He now felt like a stranger in his own country.

He knew that once he got out of prison, he would either have to reclaim his life from before or start all over again from scratch somewhere else.

There was no possible way Rhodes was returning to Newport. People still remembered him there. He was the police detective who had shot and killed a man in front of a large group of people.

His trial, although short, was the biggest news in Newport. He pleaded guilty and was sentenced immediately. This still did not stop the media from exploring all sorts of different scenarios. Some pundits argued he should be executed for what he did. Others argued he should be freed for killing a man who was ultimately found guilty of murdering a child.

At the time, Rhodes did not care what they did to him. If you asked him, his life was over. His marriage had ended, and his career was forever tarnished. If they had given him the death penalty and executed him via lethal injection, he would have accepted his fate without a fight. But his state did not have the death penalty.

The book had recommended Bridgeton as a great place to settle down for newcomers. Bridgeton got its name because it had the most bridges in the state. The city used to be an industrial hub, but during the 1970s, it lost a lot of its manufacturing jobs, leading to a mass exodus of residents.

Seeing a crisis developing, the government at the time began promoting the city as a place to raise a family. The city lowered its taxes, borrowed money, and invested in infrastructure. This led to jobs being created in the financial sector, healthcare, and education.

Bridgeton's biggest employers were banks, insurance companies, hospitals, and schools. It had gone from a down-and-out city to a city where people were better off.

However, as with any city with a large population, there was potential for crime. And Bridgeton was no different. There were regular incidents of shootings, vandalism, robberies, murders, and gang-related crimes. There were even hostage situations.

The city was a perfect place for someone like Rhodes.

As a former detective, he was wired for dealing with criminal activity. When he had picked up the newspaper at the gas station that morning, the stories he read were all crime-related. He was more interested in knowing about people on the other side of the law. They told a lot about a city.

He hoped Bridgeton would be the place he could start a new life.

He turned the corner and found himself in front of the Bridgeton Police Department.

He froze.

He was not sure why. He had not done anything wrong. He had not committed a crime. Why did he feel a knot in his stomach?

Maybe it was because he was an ex-con. Maybe it was because he used to be a member of the law. Whatever the reason, he desperately wanted to get away.

He turned around, took two steps forward, and stopped.

He closed his eyes and took a deep breath.

I am not a criminal, he reminded himself. *I've paid my debt to society. I shouldn't be afraid to enter a police station.*

He turned around and entered.

He was surprised to find the lobby empty. Perhaps it was because it was the middle of the day. Crime came alive at night.

A man was standing by the front desk. He was talking animatedly with a female officer.

Rhodes ignored them and headed to the other side of the lobby. He stopped in front of a bulletin board covered with papers. There were reward notices, wanted posters, and missing persons reports. There were too many to count.

He began scanning them. There was a notice for a missing child, a description of a suspect in a fatal shooting, and a sketch of a rapist who had attacked women in Bridgeton's downtown area.

He scanned some more.

Destruction of property. Grand larceny. Assault. You name it. It was on the board. Rhodes was more interested in the unsolved murder cases, though. Victims of robberies can recover from the loss. Victims of assault will find a way to move on. But victims of murder could neither recover nor move on.

There was also the reward money that caught his attention. Five thousand, ten thousand, and in some cases, even fifty thousand dollars for information that led to an arrest.

Rhodes knew that if a case had a financial reward attached to it, it meant the police were no closer to solving the crime, which was why they were enticing the public with money to assist them in apprehending the suspect (or suspects).

The man at the front desk got louder. "I want to speak to Detective Crowder now!"

"Stay calm, sir," the policewoman said.

"I am calm," the man replied. "My son was murdered two months ago, and so far, there have been no arrests. I want to speak to Detective Crowder."

"You can call him, sir. I can give you his number."

"I have his number and I've called him over a dozen times. He won't call me back."

"I don't know, maybe he's busy."

"He shouldn't be so busy he can't give me an update on my son's case."

"I'm sorry, sir. There is nothing I can do."

Another officer came over. "Is everything okay?"

"No, it's not," the man said. "I want to speak to Detective Jay Crowder."

Rhodes quietly left the station. He was not interested in seeing the resolution of the little drama playing out in the lobby.

ELEVEN

Jo left the subway station. Instead of driving back to the FBI field office, she decided to stop at a fast-food restaurant.

She ordered a cheeseburger, fries, and a large soft drink. It was not a healthy meal, especially for someone with a heart condition, but Jo didn't care. She had had a rough morning. A killer had walked into a busy station and left a dead body for the passengers to find. He was clearly playing a game. And he was willing to risk getting caught playing it.

He was cocky and arrogant, as well as dangerous and reckless.

What if someone had spotted him and alerted the authorities? she thought. *Would he have dropped the body and run away? Or would he have left even more dead bodies in the wake of his escape?*

It would not surprise her if the killer came armed and prepared. He would have planned for all possible outcomes. Jo did not believe his crime was a spur-of-the-moment decision.

No.

Those who committed crimes of passion often tried to hide their deeds by dumping the body in some remote area. They never disposed of the body in a public place.

But what did he hope to achieve by displaying his kill? she wondered. *Maybe it was a message? But to who? It can't be the police or FBI.*

Her eyes narrowed.

What if it was?

The killer had called the FBI field office around the time Tammy Lynn had raised the alarm. He wanted the FBI involved rather than the local police.

Her order came, and she grabbed the tray and found a seat near the window.

She pulled out the paperback Ben had given her. The title read *Killers That Got Away*.

She took a sip from her soft drink and stuffed a handful of fries in her mouth. If Dr. Cohen saw what she was eating, he would lock her away. Or, at the very least, he would have her declared unfit for duty.

She flipped the pages and found the chapter she was looking for. During the late 1980s, a serial killer had left six dead bodies underneath bridges in the city. The public had dubbed the killer the "Bridgeton Ripper." Not because the killings were somehow similar to the killings in 19th Century London, but because the killer had ripped his victim's bodies apart and then put them back together.

The author gave an overview of the case, along with a brief introduction to each of his victims. Jo chose to skip over one of the Ripper's victims. It was just too personal.

Next, the author discussed his own theories about the case. The killer, according to the author, was highly educated, perhaps even in the medical profession. The killer had to have been very patient and methodical. The victims were found cut up and stitched back together. Their organs had been removed and then placed back inside their bodies. This required extreme precision as if the killer was performing surgical procedures.

Jo was already familiar with the author's theory. She disagreed that the killer was somehow already an expert when he started his killing spree.

According to her research, the first couple of victims' bodies looked like they had been butchered. But by the time the last of the victims were found, you could not tell anything had been done to them except for minor scarring on their skin.

The killer had gone from amateur to expert.

But there was still a lot of truth to the author's theory. The killer was someone who was educated and with a medical background.

Her mind flashed back to the suspect the police believed was the Bridgeton Ripper at the time of the killings. Dagmar Kole was a cook in a small restaurant. He was uneducated and spoke very little English. Kole had come to the United States from Austria. He was a small man, but he had big hands. His family owned a butcher shop in Austria, where Kole spent his childhood learning the trade. It was easy for the police and media to believe he was capable of committing these terrible crimes. It also did not help that the police received an anonymous tip from a witness who had seen Kole on the bridge on the night the last victim's body was found and gave the police a clear description of him. It did not take long for the police to bring Kole in. He was questioned, and although he admitted he was at the bridge on that night, his statements placed him at a bridge away from the crime scene. According to Kole, a man approached him outside the restaurant he worked at and gave him one hundred dollars to pick up a package for him at that bridge.

Kole was careful with his money, and instead of taking a cab, he took a bus. Fortunately for him, he took the wrong bus and thus ended up at the wrong bridge. The bus driver later confirmed seeing Kole on that night. He looked lost and confused, not like someone who had dismembered a human being and had left their body to be found.

The police eventually let Kole go, but some of the victim's family always believed he was hiding something. Kole was never able to give an accurate description of the person who gave him the money.

The pressure from being labeled a killer was too much on the poor man. He eventually hanged himself in his apartment. An autopsy later revealed that he was suffering from the early stages of dementia.

Jo believed the real Bridgeton Ripper had tried to pin the killings on Dagmar Kole. He failed, but soon after that, the killings suddenly stopped.

Jo finished her meal and left the restaurant.

TWELVE

Jo entered the concrete and granite building and took the elevator to the sixth floor. The FBI's Bridgeton field office was in the heart of the city's downtown core. Why someone had decided to open an FBI office at this location was beyond Jo's understanding. For one thing, driving to and from the office during rush hour was a pain. Second, employees of the Bureau did not get free parking unless they were driving a government-issued vehicle.

Jo had been offered special accommodations due to her medical condition. She was given a permit that would have allowed her to park in one of the reserved spots underneath the office building. She declined. It would have meant taking a desk job if she had accepted. She would not allow her health to dictate her ability to work. She always parked in the underground parking garage of a hotel adjacent to headquarters instead.

The elevator doors opened and she got off. She headed straight for her desk, which was located in the middle of the floor.

Before she sat down, a man said, "I heard you got a nice one today."

Jo turned and found Chris Foster smiling at her. He was medium height and skinny with a mushroom-style haircut. He always wore a Hawaiian shirt. Jo once asked him why, and his response was that he dreamed of retiring to an island. Jo next asked if he had ever been to Hawaii. Chris said, no. He did not like the sun, water, or even the sand. He much preferred staying behind his computer.

Jo thought he was kidding, but he was serious.

Unlike her, Chris was not an agent. He was a civilian employee of the Bureau. He had always dreamed of working for the FBI ever since he watched the *X-Files*. However, Chris was not fit to be an agent. He was not in physical shape, and he was not particularly motivated. He was determined to work for the FBI, though. After several applications and examinations, he finally made it through and was assigned to the Bridgeton field office as an information technology expert.

"There is nothing nice about a murder," Jo replied as she sat down behind her desk.

"Yeah, but it must be cool that the killer left clues for you to piece together."

Jo sighed. "This isn't some movie, Chris."

"If the case gets more intriguing, one day it could be." His eyes suddenly lit up. "Imagine some movie studio decides to put our lives on film. Some fresh-faced starlet can play you, and Brad Pitt or George Clooney can play me."

Before Jo could respond, another man asked, "Who's playing what?"

Special Agent Tarik Habib was well-built with curly hair, tanned skin, and brown eyes. He had on V-neck sweatshirt, khaki pants, and black boots.

Jo said, "Chris thinks Brad Pitt or George Clooney would play him if they ever made a movie about us."

Tarik laughed. "They wouldn't even play your voice if they ever made an animation of you."

Chris was not amused. "That's not funny. So who would play you then?"

Tarik rubbed his chin. "If I could have someone play me, it would be Omar Sharif."

"Wasn't he an actor from the sixties?" Chris said.

"He was, but if I could have anyone play me, it would be him."

A woman walked up to them. She had on blue jeans and brown leather boots. Her top was white with a blue sports jacket over it. She had short dark hair, green eyes, and full lips.

As her rank indicated, Probationary Agent Irina Januska was still on her probation period. After her first two years were completed, she would be promoted to Special Agent.

"What're you guys talking about?" she asked in a heavy European accent.

Tarik said, "If they made a movie about us, who would you like to play you?"

"I would play me," she quickly replied.

"Have you ever acted?" Chris said.

"No, but how hard could it be?"

"It's very hard," Chris corrected her.

"It might be hard to play someone else, but it will not be hard for me to play *me*."

Chris opened his mouth but then shut it.

Jo waved her hands. "Okay, let's get back to work." She pulled out a DVD from her pocket and held it to Chris. "It's the security footage from BTA. Pull out anything you can that might help us identify the killer."

Chris snatched the DVD from her fingers. "I'm on it."

Jo turned to Tarik and Irina. "I want you guys to go to Broadview Station. The killer left the subway there, and I don't think it was random. I think he chose it for a reason. I want you to find out why."

THIRTEEN

He sat cross-legged on the floor of the spacious apartment. The apartment was located in a nice part of the city. It had floor-to-ceiling windows, a custom-built kitchen, modern furniture, and a hi-definition television.

His head was shaved and so was his face. In fact, he had gotten into the habit of shaving his entire body. He was shirtless, exposing his ripped arms, shoulders, chest and stomach. He spent as much time working out as he did meditating. There was a lot of pain and suffering in his past he never wanted to be reminded of. Meditation helped clear out the crap that was brewing in his head.

He opened his eyes and then began performing a hundred push-ups on his fists. He then proceeded to do a hundred sit-ups.

After he was drenched in sweat, he stood up and walked over to the kitchen, where he made himself a cup of herbal tea. He used to be overweight. Junk food was his best friend. Not anymore. His body was his temple, and he chose to take care of it.

He took a sip from the cup and then strolled through the apartment. He stopped at a painting in the hallway. He did not know who the artist was, but he knew the painting was expensive.

Everything in the apartment was expensive.

He could never afford a place like this. No. It was his master who was paying for this luxury.

He was just a down-on-his-luck drunk when his master had found him. He had taught him discipline. He had given him a purpose. He had saved his life.

His master had also given him a name. *Jacopo.*

He did not know what it meant, nor did he care to. His master could call him a piece of shit for all he cared.

His real name was not important, his master had told him. His real name had given him nothing but disappointment. His new name would elevate him to greater heights.

Jacopo.

The more he said that name, the more he liked it.

His master had promised him wealth in return for his obedience, and his master had not failed him. This apartment and everything inside it was his reward.

He had never come close to living in luxury. He had always been a failure. He had never been good at anything. He had gone from job to job, the last one lasting the longest: two years. His marriage had fallen apart right after that. And he had not seen his daughters in a very long time.

But he was a failure no more.

Jacopo was his name, and as Jacopo, he would live his life now.

He walked back to the living room. The television was on mute, but on the screen, a news reporter named Ellen Sheehan was talking about something. He did not need to hear her to know what she was saying. Her location told him everything.

He took another sip of his tea.

He was grateful to his master, and as his servant, he would do anything for him.

He would even kill again.

FOURTEEN

Detective Jay Crowder walked into the police station. He had short gray hair, a large belly from drinking too many beers, and his teeth had started to turn yellow from heavy smoking.

He was quickly waved over by the female officer at the front desk. "He was looking for you again," Officer Shannon said.

"Who was it?" he asked.

"You know who," Shannon replied.

Crowder grimaced. "Tim Yates?"

"Who else?"

"What did you tell him?"

"I told him you were busy. I also told him to call you."

"Good. I *was* busy."

Shannon laughed. "Sure, you were. I bet you got another lady on the side."

Crowder was twice divorced. He cheated on his first wife with his second wife and then he cheated on his second wife with his third wife. Now his third wife had caught him cheating with another woman.

"Why would you say something like that?" he asked. His eyes glinted with irritation.

Shannon scoffed. "You will bang anything that moves."

"I'm offended. And for your information, I was not with another woman. In fact, I was trying to win back my wife."

"And how did that go?"

"Not good. She won't answer my calls. She won't open the door…"

"What about your keys?"

He frowned. "She's already changed the locks."

Shannon rolled her eyes. "This is not looking good."

Crowder sighed. "I really messed up this time. I love her, and I want her back."

"What happened to the new woman?"

Crowder looked down at his belly. He shrugged. "It just didn't work out."

Shannon smirked. "I bet she realized what a mistake she had made with you and dumped your sorry butt."

He raised his arms in exasperation. "Why do you gotta kick a man when he is down?"

"Because you never learn, Jay. You keep cheating and cheating, and I'm telling you, one day, there will be no one left to cheat on. You are already old, and soon you'll be lonely."

Crowder shook his head. "I don't know why I bother talking to you."

"You talk to me because I have your back," Shannon snapped. "If I told Mr. Yates that you've been distracted with your own bullshit, he'd have you reported to the chief. How is the case going, by the way?"

"I'm working on it," he claimed, and he walked away.

Tim Yates's seventeen-year-old son, Reed, had had his cell phone stolen while he was shopping at a mall. Reed then decided to use the tracking app on the phone to locate it. But when he went to retrieve it, there was an argument and he was shot. He died a few hours later from his wounds.

When the case came to Crowder's desk, his first stop was to go the location of the shooting. It was in the parking lot of a pizza shop. Unfortunately, the shop was in a gang-infested part of the city. This meant that there were no witnesses, or at least no witnesses that were willing to come forward and give a statement.

Even the pizza shop's owner denied seeing anything. And when Crowder pressured the owner to get the security footage from the shop's cameras, he discovered the cameras were only for show, having not been in operation for years. The owner was not too concerned about being robbed either. Crowder believed one of the gangs was protecting him. He also knew no cameras meant that nothing illegal was ever recorded.

He tried using the stolen phone's GPS to locate the person behind the theft, but the feature had been disabled, leaving Crowder no electronic trail to follow. He knew he was sunk, which was why he could not bear to face Tim Yates yet.

FIFTEEN

The sun had started to set. Rhodes still did not know where he was going or what he would do next.

He had a simple plan when he had come to Bridgeton. Find a place to stay, find a place to work, and maybe start his life anew.

Daisy had nipped that plan in the bud.

He still cringed at her name. He was so gullible to fall for her damsel-in-distress story. *What if there was no boyfriend?* he had wondered later. He did not see any marks of physical abuse on her face or arms.

He shook his head. Violence toward women occurred in many ways. Just because he could not see abuse, it did not mean it was not there. Maybe Daisy had suffered from emotional abuse. But if so, why did she have to take all his money? He would have given her some if she had just asked.

Maybe she was desperate, he thought. *Maybe she saw no other way out.*

He could not ask anyone in Bridgeton for help. Maybe he could call his ex-wife and see if she would be willing to lend him some money. He would pay her back once he found some form of employment.

He shook the thought away.

There was no way he would go back to her. He had hurt her and destroyed their marriage. It took him ten years to finally be able to repay her. He was not about to ruin the good he had done in Parish.

There has to be some other way, he thought, *but what?*

Maybe he could call Tom Nolan. Nolan would send him money for sure.

Rhodes frowned. Nolan had already given him cash when Rhodes had left Franklin. He could not ask him for more.

He sighed. He could not believe he was thinking of people to hit up for cash.

Is this what my life has come to?

He never imagined he would become a pariah like his father. His father was a good-for-nothing SOB who was always sweet-talking people for money. He always promised them that he would pay them back, but he never did. Maybe he never had any intention, to begin with.

Rhodes was not like that. He did not like being in debt to anyone. Even when he was in prison, if someone did something for him, he made sure to repay them.

Rhodes looked around and realized he was in a run-down neighborhood. He walked past derelict buildings and alleys with people in sleeping bags or cardboard boxes. Rhodes could probably find a spot between them to sleep for tonight.

He was not worried about his safety. He had done time in maximum security, after all. But he was not interested in a dust-up with a druggie, pimp, or thug for encroaching on their "property."

Rhodes could go to a nicer neighborhood, though. He could find himself a park bench or even a bench in a schoolyard to sleep on. But doing so would attract attention, and that could lead to the police showing up and asking him questions or even taking him down to the station.

What if I did spend the night in jail? He thought. *It would only be for one night. In the morning, I could come up with a plan that would get me out of this jam.*

His stomach growled.

He shook his head. He was not thinking straight. Hunger was making him irrational.

There was no way in hell he would ever let himself be locked up in a cell again. He had already lost ten years of his life behind bars, and he was not going to lose a single day more. If he went hungry tonight, so be it.

As he crossed an intersection, he spotted a group of people lining up outside a building.

Rhodes could not believe his luck. He quickened his pace and joined them.

SIXTEEN

Tarik and Irina returned to the office.

"You find anything?" Jo asked.

"We canvassed the area around Broadview Station," Tarik said. "There is a convenience store across the station with CCTV cameras. The owner wasn't willing to let us see the footage."

"Why not?" Jo asked.

Irina said, "He was probably selling cigarettes to minors and was worried we might see something that could incriminate him."

"We assured him that we were only interested in the camera outside the store and not the one inside," Tarik said.

"Did you get it?" Jo said.

Tarik pulled out a DVD.

Chris appeared from out of nowhere and grabbed the disc.

"Where did you come from?" Tarik asked, surprised.

"I'm like a rare Siberian tiger. I can appear and disappear at will."

"I wish *you* would just disappear."

"Very funny. I know you don't mean that," Chris said, inserting the DVD into his laptop. He pulled up the footage on a giant monitor.

Chris already knew the time the killer had walked out of the station. He had already gone through the footage from BTA. He scrolled through the new footage and let it play.

Jo, Tarik, and Irina huddled around the monitor to get a better view.

The camera was facing the exterior of the convenience store, but they could see the subway station entrance across the street.

"Can you zoom in?" Jo asked.

"I can do more than that," Chris replied. The image became enlarged and distorted, but after Chris tapped a few keys, the image became more focused. "I've manipulated the pixels," Chris explained.

They saw people enter and exit the station. A few tedious minutes went by before Jo said, "There!"

A man walked through the front doors. He was wearing a jacket, hoodie and baseball cap. He kept his head low as if he was avoiding being photographed by a camera.

He left the station and walked down the street. His image became blurry.

"Zoom in more," Jo said.

"I'll try, but the camera isn't set up to catch that angle," Chris replied.

The image zoomed in some more, but it was still not enough to get a clear view of the man. They watched as he got in a parked car and drove away.

"Can we catch the license plate?" Jo asked.

Chris shook his head. "It's too far."

Jo turned to Tarik and Irina. "Any businesses in that area?"

Tarik shook his head. "No. There's only a park."

Jo frowned. "It must be why the killer chose to leave his car there. He must have checked the area out beforehand. I knew there was a reason why he exited the subway at Broadview."

"So we got nothing," Chris said. He sounded deeply disappointed.

"Not exactly," Tarik replied.

They turned to him.

"We might not know the license plate, but I can tell you the car was a Mercedes-Benz S Class."

"How can you tell that?" Irina asked.

"I have a similar model at home."

"How much do they go for?" Chis asked.

"Starting price is around ninety-five thousand," Tarik said.

"How can you afford one?"

Irina said, "He's got a rich family back in Egypt."

Tarik was born in the U.S., but when he was five years old, his father moved back to Egypt to run the family's import and export business. His father hoped that once Tarik had completed his studies, he would return to Egypt and take over the family business. Tarik had other plans. He wanted to get into law enforcement. This caused a strain in his relationship with his parents. To make matters more complicated, Tarik was a Coptic Christian, and he married a Catholic. His parents never approved of the union. However, things were better now. His younger brother had taken over more of the family responsibilities. Plus, with his wife now pregnant, his parents were more than willing to let bygones be bygones with a grandchild on the way.

The Mercedes was their olive branch to him.

"My family's rich, but I'm not," Tarik corrected Irina.

"Whatever, you have a Mercedes. I drive a beat-up Kia."

Chris turned to her. "I don't own a car, but if you want, we can buy a new car together."

Irina crossed her arms over her chest. "And why would I do that with *you*?"

"I mean, after you've fallen madly in love with me, it'll be convenient for both of us to come to work in the same car, right?"

Irina rolled her eyes. "No chance in hell that's ever going to happen."

"Never say never," Chris said. "I never thought I'd be struck by lightning, but it happened twice."

Tarik couldn't help but jump in. "I knew there was a reason why something was wrong with you."

Jo had heard enough banter. She grabbed her jacket. "I'm out of here. I'll see you guys tomorrow."

SEVENTEEN

Rhodes found a seat in the corner and quickly began devouring his meal. He was at the House of Hope, a soup kitchen for the homeless and destitute.

The House of Hope was located in the basement of a church. The room could fit almost thirty people, and right now, it was filled to capacity. The diners were mostly men, with a few women sprinkled amongst them. They were ragged and filthy and some stank. The volunteers were oblivious to the conditions of their patrons, however. They smiled at each person in line and handed them a paper plate with corn, mashed potatoes, a slice of bread, and a piece of meat. Rhodes wasn't sure what the meat was, but it tasted really good.

Standing in line reminded him of his time in prison, where he would line up with all the inmates and wait for his tray to be filled with whatever was on the menu for that day. The food did not vary from day to day, but during the holidays, they would be treated with something extra: a piece of turkey on Thanksgiving, a slice of fruitcake on Christmas, or extra eggs on Easter. These were not decadent items, but after weeks of eating bland meals, anything different was welcomed.

Rhodes was not a stickler when it came to food. He only cared that he had enough for his stomach. At the beginning of his sentence, he would let other inmates take some of his meal without protest. They would take his bread. They would eat a spoonful of his potatoes. They would even snatch his entire tray.

Rhodes quickly realized they were not stealing from him because they were hungry. They were stealing because they were bored. After being locked up for most of the day, they looked forward to interacting with other inmates. A dust-up with another inmate in the prison cafeteria was the highlight of their day.

Rhodes put an end to the thievery. The next time an inmate came up to steal his meal, Rhodes would use the tray, a spoon, or whatever else he had to hurt the inmate. This sent him to isolation, but the altercation sent the offending inmate to isolation as well. To hammer his point across, every time he saw the inmate who attempted to take his meal, Rhodes would go up and take his first. The altercation would again send them both to isolation, but this taught everyone around him a lesson: *If you mess with me, be prepared to be messed with for a long time after.*

A man came up and sat across from him. He was short and slim with a boyish face and red hair. He wore a clerical collar.

"You're not from around here, are you?" he asked.

Rhodes shook his head. He wanted to say he was just passing by, but that would not be true.

"We don't normally see new faces," the priest said. "We know all the regulars, those who come day after day for a hot meal. These people have nowhere else to go, but you look like someone who does."

"I hate to admit it, but I don't."

"I see." The priest nodded. "One day you have a warm bed and the next day you don't. I see a lot of people who've been there. Some lost their jobs, or their marriage ended, or they made bad business decisions, had a gambling habit, or got hooked on drugs."

Rhodes wanted to tell the priest that he was not like the other people there. He was just going through a period of bad luck. Maybe they were too if he thought about it. Theirs just lasted longer.

"By the way, they call me Father Mike," the priest said.

"Martin Rhodes," Rhodes replied.

Father Mike squinted. "I think I read about you in a newspaper. You wouldn't be from Newport, would you?"

Rhodes suddenly regretted giving his full name. He could have called himself John, or Frank, or Joe, and the priest would not have been the wiser. Rhodes worried the priest would kick him out for being a murderer.

Instead, Father Mike smiled. "We don't judge people here. I won't condone what you did, but I won't admonish you for it either."

Rhodes stared at him and then finished his meal.

Father Mike said, "A lot of these people only come here to eat. They'll be back out on the streets once they are fed. We have beds upstairs for them, but they don't want to adhere to our rules."

"What rules are those?" Rhodes inquired.

"No fighting, no drugs, and lights out at midnight. In the morning, they have to be up at six, and after a simple breakfast, they have to leave. We just don't have the resources to let them make the House of Hope their permanent place of residence, you know."

"I can live by those rules," Rhodes offered.

Father Mike smiled. "Then you are welcome to stay the night."

EIGHTEEN

Jo was over at her brother's house for dinner almost every other day, and today was one of those occasions. The moment she walked in the front door, she heard a voice say, "Aunty Jo is here! Aunty Jo is here!"

Two seconds later, a girl wearing a blue dress came running over. Jo grabbed her and lifted her up in the air. Chrissy was four, and she was Jo's niece.

"How are you, sweetie?" Jo said, hugging her tightly.

"I'm good."

"And what dress are you wearing?"

"Mommy bought it for me. It's a fairy princess dress."

"Is it really?"

"Yeah, and I wore it to school and everyone told me it looked beautiful. I got so tired of saying 'thank you.'" She let out a loud sigh, as if being showered with compliments was the most exhausting thing ever.

"Well, you do look beautiful," Jo said.

Chrissy beamed. "I know."

Jo put Chrissy down and found her sister-in-law in the kitchen. Kim Davis-Pullinger had on an apron and was standing behind the stove. Her hair was straight, her skin was black, and she had an amazing smile.

Jo walked over and kissed her on the cheek.

"Dinner is almost ready," Kim said.

"I know I was supposed to come early and help, but we got a case that tied me up," Jo said.

"I hope it's not the one on the news."

"It is."

"Get out. Really?" Kim asked, shocked.

"Yep."

"Did they really find him without his hands?"

"How did you know about that?" Jo asked.

"I have internet, you know."

"I can't confirm nor deny it, but yes."

Both women laughed.

"Where's Sam?" Jo asked

"He's in the backyard, clearing out the leaves. Can you tell him dinner is almost ready?"

"Sure."

Samuel Pullinger was two years older than Jo. He was completely bald. He started losing his hair in his twenties and had shaved his head ever since. He was tall and thin, and he wore wire-rimmed glasses.

Sam worked for the government as a forensic accountant. He had met Kim at his job. Sam specialized in financial crimes that involved monitoring securities, digital currencies, credit cards, and even traditional currency.

"Dinner will be ready soon," Jo said.

Sam nodded, but kept raking.

"You need any help?" she asked.

"I'm almost done," he replied. He raked the leaves into a pile and began putting them in a giant paper bag.

Jo pulled out the book that Ben had given her and said, "I found some more information on the Bridgeton Ripper case."

Sam did not say anything.

"Aren't you interested?" she said.

"Do you know who the Bridgeton Ripper is?" he asked.

She shook her head.

"Then I'm not interested."

"You don't even want to read it?"

He finally looked at her. "No, Jo. I don't. And you shouldn't either. It was over twenty years ago. You have to let it go and move on with your life."

Jo looked away.

His voice softened. "You know I didn't mean it like that."

She looked down at her feet.

"You haven't visited mom for a couple of weeks," he said.

"I know. I've just been busy."

"You should see her. It'll make her feel better."

"I will, but it's not like she knows I'm even there."

"You don't know that. Everyone needs love and affection, even if they are incapable of showing it."

"You were always closer to mom than I was," Jo said.

"And you were closer to dad, but that doesn't mean I don't miss him."

Jo nodded. "I'll go for sure. I promise."

After Sam had filled the bag with leaves, he said, "How are you feeling?"

There were not a lot of people who knew of Jo's heart condition, but Sam and Kim did. They were family, after all.

"I had a bit of a scare in the morning," she confessed.

"And did you go see Dr. Cohen?" he asked.

"I did."

Sam looked at her. "And did he tell you to think about getting a transplant?"

She knew where this was going. "No, he didn't. In fact, he said I should focus on finding who the Bridgeton Ripper is, and when I catch him, my heart will be completely healed."

Sam frowned at her. "It's not funny, Jo. I worry about you. With mom the way she is, you're the only family I've got."

"What about Kim and Chrissy?"

"You know what I mean."

Jo walked over and gave him a hug.

"I love you, Sam," she said.

"I love you too," he replied.

The back door opened and Kim said, "I know you guys are having a brother-and-sister moment, but dinner is getting cold."

Chrissy said from behind her, "Come and have your dinner, Aunty Jo. We have chocolate cake for dessert."

Chrissy loved sweets. She would badger Jo to finish her dinner quickly so her mom could bring out the dessert.

"Alright," Jo said. "But you better not rush me, or else I'll eat very slowly."

"I promise I won't, but hurry up."

Jo smiled. Kids never changed.

NINETEEN

Ellen Sheehan was at BN-24's headquarters. It was five-thirty in the morning, and she was not sure why her boss had called her into the station so early.

She had her phone in one hand and a large decaf in the other. She was able to apply some makeup on her drive over. It was technically illegal in Bridgeton to call, text, or even put on lipstick while you were driving, but Ellen always figured no cops were paying attention so early in the morning.

Ellen had been pulled over for driving while distracted, but she always managed to get out of a ticket by telling the officer that she was on her way to a breaking story. Some cops would still insist on going through the entire process of checking her license and insurance, but she would make it look like she had received a call from her producer. She would tell her imaginary producer that she could not cover the story because officer—she would then ask for his or her name—would not let her go with a warning. She would end the call by saying she was sorry that thousands of viewers would be disappointed with the broadcast tonight, but the law was the law. When she would finally hang up, the officer would hand over her information and tell her to be careful in the future. Her ploy always worked, and she doubted it would ever fail.

She was seated on a comfy leather sofa in her producer's office. Miles Stevens was on the phone behind his desk. He had tanned skin, dark hair, and a square jawline. His eyes were always focused, and when he spoke to you, it looked like he was staring directly into your soul.

Stevens was not even thirty-five when he was promoted to run the 24-hour news station. He was ambitious and highly motivated. He rarely gave compliments, and when he called someone in his office, it was usually to give them the bad news.

Ellen was not worried, though. Her coverage of the body on the train had gotten a positive response from the public. Her social media page was flooded with comments and feedback from viewers. Her blog on the BN-24 website had gotten over five thousand hits just in the last twelve hours.

Ellen smiled. Her coverage focused not only on the murder but also on how it affected Bridgeton's commuters. This had struck a chord with the viewers. Social networking sites were flooded with complaints from riders about not being able to find alternative modes of transportation whenever the transit system shut down. BTA was always ill-prepared to handle the major complications that hit the system.

BTA, in their defense, blamed the mayor for not spending more money on transit. They were forced to utilize a system that relied on old buses and trains that were now becoming antiques. The cost of maintaining them was becoming astronomical. The tracks, the stations, even the collection booths, were outdated. The system needed an overhaul.

The question then came down to who would pay for the system's rehabilitation. Surely not the public. Any hint of raising taxes to support transit infrastructure caused approval ratings to spiral downwards. No politician dared tackle the issue out of fear of being booted out of office.

Thus, the transit system would continue to be on life support until the day when some brave politician chose to make it his or her main focus, or when the system was sold to a private enterprise to be run as they chose.

Regardless of the outcome, Ellen was happy that her story had sparked a debate.

Miles hung up the phone and said, "Sorry about that. It was my boss."

She's up this early too? Ellen thought. "So why am I here, Miles?"

"You know I think you did a wonderful job on the train story, right?"

She did not like the sound of that. "But…"

"But, my boss wants someone else to take over."

"No way!" Ellen jumped up. "That's *my* story!"

Miles put his hands up. "Relax. Sit down. Hear me out."

Ellen sat down and crossed her arms over her chest.

Miles said, "While your coverage was great, we got hammered by SUNTV. Janie Fernandez hit the story out of the ballpark."

Ellen curled her lips. *That slut.*

"It's a big story," Miles said. "It's not every day that a body is found on the subway, especially not one where the victim's hands are cut off." The FBI had already briefed the media on some aspects of the case. Ellen still felt they were withholding vital information, and she wanted to force them to divulge it.

"Did you see my social media page?" Ellen held up her phone. "My story's got a thousand thumbs-ups, and it's trending all over the internet."

"I know, but that doesn't make this station money. Ad money does. And that comes from ratings. On the six o'clock news, Janie's segment beat your segment by a longshot. I hate to say it, but you came across as desperate and bitter."

"What is that supposed to mean?" Ellen shot back.

"It means you can't let your animosity for Janie get to you. It showed on the screen. The camera doesn't lie."

Ellen scoffed. "This is bullshit, you know."

Miles let her stew for a bit.

"So who's taking over *my* story," Ellen finally asked.

"Dan Ferguson."

Ellen's mouth dropped. "Dan retired last year."

"Well, he's bored, and he wants to come back on a part-time basis. Dan's a veteran at this. Viewers respect him."

"They will respect me, too, if you let me do my story."

"I'm not going to argue with you, Ellen. My boss thinks it's a good idea, and I think it's a good idea too. But to make it up to you, I'll let you decide what story to cover next."

Ellen sighed. Her shoulders sagged. "Okay, what are they?"

"The opening of a new fitness center, or the end of a long-running stage show. It's your pick."

Ellen knew both were frivolous stories, but she clearly had no choice in the matter. "I'll take the fitness center. I can't stand talking to those artsy-fartsy actors."

Miles smiled. "Great. I already called Walt. He should be down here soon."

Ellen stood up. As she made her way to the door, she stopped and turned to Miles. "One of these days, a big story will fall into my lap, and you'll have no choice but to let *me* cover it."

She stormed out of the office.

TWENTY

When Jo arrived at the office, she found Chris sitting behind her desk. "How long have you been there?" she inquired.

"Not long," he replied.

"And why are you in my chair?"

"I've been waiting for you, Miss Pullinger." Chris tapped his fingers together, and his lips curled into a smile.

Jo knew whenever Chris found something. He would start re-enacting scenes from his favorite science fiction movies. Sometimes Chris was the hero, other times, he was the villain. She suddenly realized that Chris preferred being the villain more than the hero. Maybe villains were more exciting? She couldn't imagine why.

"Okay, what have you got for me?" she said.

He lowered his voice. "What I'm about to tell you will forever change your life. If you drink from the red glass, your world will open up to unimaginable possibilities. If you drink from the blue glass, your world will stay the same."

Jo rolled her eyes. "You know what? I'll drink from the blue cup…"

"Glass."

"Glass, cup, whatever. Get off my desk before I shoot you."

"I can dodge bullets, you know."

"Dodge this." Her hand went to her holster. Chris immediately jumped up from the chair.

"You're no fun," he complained.

She smiled. "Seeing you jump like a rabbit was fun."

"Okay, I'll tell you what I've found."

She sat down and faced him.

"I ran the victim's photo through our facial recognition software and got a hit."

"And who is he?" Jo asked.

"Silvio Tarconi." Chris pulled out a six-by-eight photo and handed it to her. Tarconi had a frown. His hair was disheveled, and his eyes were glazed. "A year ago, he was arrested for a misdemeanor assault outside a bar. His blood alcohol was twice the legal limit. He said he didn't remember what happened. I bet he didn't." Chris pulled out a sheet of paper. "That's his address."

Jo quickly got up. "Find out anything else you can on him."

***

The apartment building looked nice from the outside but became something else the moment Jo stepped inside. She could tell the building was run by the city's social housing program. The program was heavily underfunded, leaving many buildings neglected and in dire shape. This had caused an uproar a few years back, with citizens picketing outside the mayor's office.

Instead of infusing more money and rebuilding the housing projects, the city instead opted to only renovate the exterior of the buildings. They were not concerned with what the tenants in the building thought. They were low-income citizens who hardly ever voted, so their opinions held no weight to the politicians. The renovations were done for the average citizen who could pass by a building like this without knowing how bad it was inside.

Jo waited for the elevator but realized that out of the three, only one was working. She decided to take the stairs. Fortunately, Tarconi lived on the third floor, so the walk up didn't put too much stress on her heart.

She found the apartment and unlocked the door with a key she had picked up from the superintendent. Even run-down buildings had someone responsible for their upkeep. The superintendent had not been paid for months, but he was still helpful, nonetheless.

She flicked on the hall light and moved inside the apartment. There was a kitchen to the left. The garbage bin was overflowing, and dirty dishes were piled high in the sink. There were fruit flies everywhere.

It looked like Tarconi was not big on cleanliness.

The living room was no better. The sofa was worn with stain marks everywhere. In some places, the wool was sticking out. The coffee table was completely filled with beer bottles, old magazines, and newspapers. And there was an ashtray full of stubbed out cigarette butts.

She sensed movement behind her.

She immediately reached for her gun. She relaxed when she saw a gray cat stick its head out from the bedroom.

The cat stared at her and then moved to the kitchen. He licked at an empty tray on the floor. Jo went to the kitchen and rummaged through the cabinets until she found a bag of cat food. She filled the tray and headed for the bedroom.

She stopped and took a peek inside the bathroom. The smell deterred her from going in.

The bedroom had a mattress on the floor, which was covered in old laundry. Next to the mattress were rolled up joints of weed and a bong. Jo spotted more bottles of beer and some medication bottles. She leaned down and saw that the latter were painkillers.

She went back out to the living room. Next to the television cabinet was a side table. On it were several envelopes. There were letters from the disability office, from social assistance corporations, and even some from marketing companies.

Jo quickly went through the pile until she spotted something underneath it. She picked the object up. It was an ID card from the Bridgeton Mental Care Institute. Tarconi had not changed much from the photo on the card, even though it was dated five years earlier.

She walked to the middle of the living room and surveyed the area. How did a man living on disability checks end up dead on a train? And why were his hands cut off and the words WHAT THE HANDS TOUCH carved on his chest?

It did not make any sense to her.

Tarconi lived alone, save for his cat. From the way he kept his apartment, Jo could tell he did not get many visitors, either. Plus, he was unemployed.

Who did he piss off so badly that they wanted to not only kill him but leave his body for others to find?

Jo had no idea. And spending time inside the filthy and smelly apartment was not helping her find any answers either.

The cat had already gone through the bowl. Jo picked him up and walked out of the apartment. She would drop the cat off at an animal shelter while she was on her way back to the office.

TWENTY-ONE

Rhodes felt refreshed after a good night's sleep. He could not say that same for his roommates. Almost all were suffering from some form of ailment. One coughed all night. Another would have fits during his sleep. The person next to him snored constantly.

Through it all, Rhodes did not wake up once. It was something he had learned in prison. The first couple of nights were terrible, he remembered. He would spend them wide awake. The noise in his cell block was too much to ignore. It felt like the walls amped up each sound. If someone coughed, it could be heard throughout the cell block. If someone moaned or cried or even mumbled, it could be heard inside multiple cells.

He had tried to cover his ears with a pillow or blanket. He even went as far as to stuff toilet paper in his ears, but after many sleepless nights, he was able to tune the noise out.

Maybe he was just tired like he was the night before. After spending most of the day walking the city, he was exhausted.

He was up before Father Mike came to wake everyone up. He was able to shower and shave, and then he went to breakfast, which consisted of a selection of coffee, tea, bagels, toast, or egg sandwiches. Rhodes opted for the coffee and the sandwich. They both were warm and filled his stomach.

While Rhodes was on his way out, Father Mike reminded him that he was welcome to come back. Rhodes thanked him for the offer, but he knew he could not keep going back to the shelter. It was a short-term solution. He needed something long-term. And in order to do that, he needed a job.

As he walked the streets once again, he realized he never had a plan on how to get employment when he came to Bridgeton. He figured the money he was bringing with him would last a couple of months or maybe longer. This would give him enough time to get a feel for the city. *I will eventually find something to do*, he had told himself.

Now things were different. He had to start earning some cash soon. Without money, he would be returning to the House of Hope every night.

There was another reason Rhodes did not want to do that. He was taking a bed from someone who genuinely needed it. There were people there who were in worse situations than him. They were mentally or physically ill. Some were battling addictions.

Without the House of Hope, they would be on the streets, surrounded by drugs and alcohol. The House of Hope not only gave them a meal but also a warm place to stay, and more importantly, it gave them hope.

Rhodes turned the corner and suddenly stopped. He was once again in front of the police station.

It finally dawned on him why he kept passing it.

Most of the homeless had criminal records and many were in and out of prison, so it made sense to open a shelter near a police station.

Rhodes did not know why, but something made him want to go inside again. Maybe he was feeling nostalgic about his time as a detective.

He followed his instinct and stepped through the front entrance.

He headed straight to the bulletin board. The notices had not changed from the day before. It was sad, really. He wished someone would provide closure to all these families, whether it was finding someone's missing child, finding the person who was responsible for a death in their family, or even just telling the family that their loved one would never return. He felt this was an important part of the grieving process.

"You lose someone too?" a voice asked from behind him.

Rhodes turned and realized it was the same man he had seen here yesterday.

Rhodes shook his head.

"Hey, weren't you here yesterday?" the man asked.

Rhodes nodded. *I should leave*, he thought. He was surprised the man had seen him or even remembered him. He had been too busy giving the officer at the desk a hard time.

The man pointed at a photo on the bulletin board. "That's my son," the man said.

Rhodes leaned over. *Reed Yates*. He was seventeen. He wore round glasses, and his teeth were girded with braces. In the photo, he wore a suit, which told Rhodes it was probably taken at a wedding.

The man said, "Reed was a good kid. He wanted to follow in my footsteps. He wanted to go to Columbia. He wanted to become an architect like me." He looked at Rhodes. "I've got a much younger daughter, but she's more like her mother. Reed? He was just like me. He was my future. I loved him so much."

The man's eyes moistened.

Rhodes finally said, "You should get your lawyer to write to the police board. As the family of a murdered victim, you have every right to get an update on your son's case. In fact, you can also contact a victim advocacy group. I'm sure there are good ones in Bridgeton."

The man looked confused.

"I heard you talking to the lady at the desk the other day," Rhodes explained.

The man nodded. "Are you a police officer?"

"I used to be."

"What do you do now?"

"I'm new in Bridgeton."

"So, are you looking for a job?"

Rhodes paused.

The man pointed at his son's notice. "There is a ten thousand dollar reward for anyone who provides information that leads to an arrest. I put up that money. If you help me find who killed my son, I will double the reward for you."

Rhodes stared at him for almost a minute. He shook his head. "I'm sorry. I don't know how I can help you. I'm just a civilian now."

"What did you do when you worked for the police?" the man asked.

Rhodes knew where this was going, but he did not want to lie. "I was a detective."

The man's eyes lit up. "Then, you have to help me."

Rhodes was not sure. "What's the guarantee I'll be able to find anything if the police haven't found it yet?"

"To them, Reed is just another homicide victim, one of maybe a dozen or even hundreds in the city. But in your case, he'll be your only focus."

Rhodes hesitated.

"I'll even give you an advance."

Rhodes bit his bottom lip. He was desperate for money. He did not want to line up again at the House of Hope.

"My name is Tim Yates, by the way."

"Martin... Martin Rhodes."

"Mr. Rhodes, you have to help me, please," Yates said. "Do you have any children?"

Rhodes shook his head.

"I was going to say if you did, then you would know what it feels like losing a child."

Rhodes paused. It was a father who had shot and killed his young son. Rhodes had shot the father in reprisal and went to prison.

Tim Yates was a father whose situation was the exact opposite.

"Okay, but on two conditions," Rhodes said.

"Name them."

"I need five thousand in advance."

The man frowned. "That's a lot of money up front."

"I don't have a place to stay, and I don't even have a mode of personal transportation. I need money to get settled and then I can start work."

"Okay, fine. What the second condition?"

"Get the file the police have on your son's case. I want to see everything. When you have the file, meet me at the bar down the street."

TWENTY-TWO

Rhodes was at the bar an hour before Tim Yates was supposed to arrive. He was certain Yates would come. He had to believe that. Rhodes did not have the money for the beer he held in his hand. If Yates failed to show up, well, Rhodes and the bartender would have a long discussion.

Rhodes knew it would not come to that. Yates was desperate, and he would do anything to find who killed his son.

Rhodes just was not sure he was the right man for the job. He had no badge and no resources to conduct an investigation with. All he could do was examine the facts the police had gathered and come to a conclusion. He would further investigate anything the police may have overlooked, but in his experience, the chances of that happening were slim.

The detective on the case would have already followed up on all leads. If those leads did not lead to a suspect, the case had turned cold.

It was rare that evidence suddenly popped up unexpectedly. It did happen, though. A witness grew a conscience and came forward to the police. A worker discovered something pertinent to the case while performing his job. An accomplice who was bitter with the killer gave him up out of spite. But all these happenings occurred due to forces beyond the detective's investigative powers.

Rhodes took a slow sip from his glass. It was almost half empty. Rhodes hoped Yates would arrive before he took his last sip.

The bar's door swung open and two men came in. They looked around and then came over. They sat on the stools on either side of Rhodes.

"Well, well, well, if it isn't Marty Rhodes," the one on his right said.

Rhodes turned and looked at him. The man was heavy with a shaved head, and he had a long handlebar mustache.

The other said, "You are right, Barry. It is Marty Rhodes." He was big with broad shoulders, and a scar ran down his left cheek.

Rhodes squinted. He was not sure who either of them was.

The first man smiled, revealing his gold tooth. "Forgotten me already, have ya?" He then slapped Rhodes on the shoulder.

Rhodes's back tensed, and his fist tightened. He was ready to give him a piece of his mind, but as there were two of them, he let the situation play out.

"It's your Uncle Barry."

Rhodes's eyes widened. Barry Kowalski was a friend of Rhodes's father. Rhodes had not seen Barry since he last spoke to his father, which was years ago.

"You still robbing banks?" Rhodes asked.

Barry laughed. "That was the old times, boy. Now, like the banks, I loan money out to desperate people."

"What do you want?" Rhodes asked, realizing he wanted very little to do with him or his buddy.

Barry leaned over. Rhodes could smell his foul breath. "You see, your dad owes me a lot of money. Heck, he owes a lot of people a lot of money. But seeing that we were buddies way back, I've been giving him a free pass. The interest on his loans is so low that even the banks would think I'm crazy. All I'm asking is that he pays me back what he owes me. That's it."

"Why are you telling me this?" Rhodes asked.

"He said you'd have the money."

"He did?"

Barry smiled. "Yep."

"And you believed him?"

"Of course not. I trust your dad as much as he trusts me, which is not saying much. I actually wanted to see you, Marty. I guess the apple didn't fall too far from the tree."

Rhodes knew he was referring to his time in prison. The inference irritated him.

Rhodes said, "I don't have any money."

Barry stood up. "Well, that's too bad, because now I'd have to put our history aside and do something really bad to your dad."

"How much does he owe you?" Rhodes blurted out. He quickly regretted his words.

"Three grand."

Rhodes sighed. "Give me some time. Let me see what I can do."

"I knew it." Barry laughed and slapped him on the shoulder again. "You were always a good kid, you know that."

Barry and his goon left the bar.

TWENTY-THREE

Rhodes was furious. He could not believe his dad was pulling him into his problems. He always did that. Although when Rhodes was a detective, his father stayed away from him. He had made some attempts to contact his son, but they were too few to count. Rhodes believed his father was worried his criminal lifestyle would force Rhodes to take action against him.

His father knew how much Rhodes despised him. If given a chance, Rhodes would not have hesitated to throw his dad in jail. It was better if he stayed away from his son.

Now that Rhodes was no longer a detective or in prison, his father somehow wanted him back in his life.

Rhodes would deal with him when the time came. Right now, he had a job to worry about.

He watched as Tim Yates entered the bar, looked around, spotted him, and came over.

Rhodes held up his glass. "Do you mind paying the bartender for the drink?"

"Sure," said Yates.

When his tab was paid, Rhodes took him to a corner booth by the windows.

Once they were seated, Yates said, "You were right. When my lawyer sent a letter straight to the chief's office, Detective Crowder had no choice but to let me see how far he'd gotten on the case." He slid over a thin file. "I'm afraid he didn't get too far."

Rhodes did not flip it open. He just tapped it with his index finger.

Yates understood. He slid over a thick white envelope.

Rhodes did not touch it. "I want you to know something. I was convicted of murder and spent ten years in prison for it."

"I know who you are," Yates replied. "I did an internet search on you before I came down. I read the article from the Franklin *Daily Times*. That reporter, Hyder Ali, wrote a detailed piece on you. It told me everything I needed to know."

Rhodes said, "Then you know that with my background, I'm not allowed to perform services as a private investigator."

"I didn't know that, but if anyone asked, I'll say I paid you for consulting services."

"Consulting?"

"Sure. I'm getting an outside opinion from a former police detective on my son's case. That's it."

Rhodes mulled Yate's words over. Without looking inside the envelope, he put it in his pocket.

"I'll start work right away," Rhodes said.

"How will I find you?" Yates asked.

"I'll find you."

Rhodes stood up.

Yates put his hand on his arm. Rhodes glared at him. Yates quickly let go. "I'm sorry, but this is about my son. I hope you won't disappoint me."

"I promise I will do *everything* I can to find the person responsible for your son's death. But I can't promise you that I will be successful."

"I can live with that."

TWENTY-FOUR

Jo was at her desk when Irina came over.

"I spoke to the neighbors, and they all said the victim was a quiet guy. He kept to himself and didn't really interact with anyone. He used to be in a relationship, but that was a long time ago."

After her visit to Silvio Tarconi's apartment, Jo had sent Irina to find out more about him.

"How did the neighbors know he used to be in a relationship?" Jo asked.

"They used to see him with a woman."

"Did they know who she was?"

"I asked the neighbors, but they had no idea."

"How long ago was it?"

"Almost three years."

Jo frowned. "That doesn't help. But it makes sense why no one reported him missing."

Irina said, "I also spoke to the rental company, and they said they never had any problems with him. He paid his rent on time, and he never caused any trouble. Even his neighbors agree they never had any disputes with him."

"So he was a good tenant and a good neighbor. Then why was he targeted?" Jo wondered aloud.

Tarik came over. "I did some digging on the victim's family."

"And?" Jo asked.

"Nothing that will help us, I'm afraid. He was an only child, and his parents died when he was young. His grandmother raised him, and she passed away ten years ago."

Jo said, "No family. No friends. No relationships. It doesn't make any sense."

"How so?" Tarik asked.

"If the killer chose a victim no one would miss, then why leave his body on the train with a message on it? The killer *was* making an example of Tarconi, which I'm sure of. But why?"

Chris suddenly appeared and said, "You guys are having a party. Why am I not invited?"

"We're not having a party," Irina said. "We're discussing the case."

"It's a joke," Chris replied. "Don't you guys joke back in Russia?"

"I'm from Ukraine."

"Same thing."

Irina's face turned red. "No, it's not."

"It is. Russian and Ukrainian women are hot. Same thing."

"Have you ever been to Russia?" she asked.

"As a matter of fact, I have."

Irina was surprised. "When?"

"When I was a baby. My parents took me with them."

"That doesn't count."

Chris shrugged. "Hey, I was there. I just don't remember my visit." He leaned closer to her. "If you want to take me to Ukraine and meet your mom, I'm all for it."

Irina had come to the U.S. on a student visa. After completing her studies, she decided to apply for immigration. Once she received her U.S. citizenship, she applied to the academy and got in. She had a mother in Ukraine. She supported her by sending her money. Irina's hope was that once she became a full-time special agent, she would try to sponsor her mother's immigration.

"Why would I want you to meet my mother?" she asked.

"I mean, once we are dating, I should meet your family, you know."

Irina frowned. "You're not my type."

"What's wrong with me?" Chris asked. "I have a job and I live by myself."

"No, you don't," Irina corrected him. "You live in your parent's house."

"They are in Florida most of the year, so I technically live by myself."

"It doesn't count."

"It's a big house. There's room for everyone." He winked at her.

"I feel sick," she said.

"Okay, so who's your type?" he asked.

She thought about it. "You ever watch the show *American Sport Challenge*?"

Chris shook his head. "Never heard of it."

Jo said, "Neither have I."

Tarik said, "I have. It's a show where men and women go through a series of extreme obstacle courses."

Irina nodded. "I'm training to one day compete in it. If you got on that show, I would go out with you."

Chris let out a mock laugh. "No problem. How hard could it be?"

Tarik put a hand on his shoulder. "Don't even think about it. Even *I* won't be able to get through one of the obstacles."

Chris stared at him. Tarik was in far better shape than he was. He took a big gulp and then walked away before his big mouth got him in deeper trouble.

TWENTY-FIVE

Ellen watched as the man cut the donut in half. He placed a grilled piece of meat in the middle. He covered it up with two strips of bacon and a slice of cheese. He then proceeded to fry the entire donut burger.

Ellen wanted to gag.

She was at the opening of a new restaurant where the food was made to clog your arteries. The chef was a man in his late thirties. He had a bushy beard, his hair was tied in a ponytail, and his arms were covered in tattoos.

Ellen could tell Walt was salivating. *Men and their fried foods*, she thought.

"I call this a heart attack waiting to happen," the chef said.

No kidding, Ellen wanted to say. She smiled at him, but it was mostly for the camera. "So, how has the response been since you opened up?"

She shoved the microphone closer to his bushy face.

"It's been great," he replied with enthusiasm. "We can't keep up with the demand."

Ellen had to stop herself from rolling her eyes. She had been at the restaurant for almost an hour, and so far, she had only seen two customers walk in. Neither had bought anything. They were just curious to see what was on the menu. When they saw items such as deep-fried butter covered in batter, or a deep-fried chocolate bar eaten in a bagel, or even deep-fried waffle sandwiches stuffed with French fries, Ellen could not blame them for leaving.

She did feel sorry for the chef, though. Before opening the restaurant, he had worked as an investment banker. After years of advising people to follow their dreams, he decided to quit his secure job and invest all his life savings in a dream of his own.

Ellen felt sorry for herself too. She could not believe she had let Miles talk her into letting Dan Ferguson cover *her* story. *She* should have been following up on all the leads, not Dan. In fact, Dan should have been the one watching this idiot destroy his life. Why would you throw money into a business that was nothing but a novelty? Surely, people would not keep coming back every day to have the same heart-attack-inducing meal? It was just plain stupid.

Ellen watched as the chef let the donut burger bubble and simmer in the hot oil.

She wanted to yell, *Take it out! It's burnt enough*. Instead, she asked with a smile, "How long do you let it cook?"

"Until it's hard and crispy," the chef replied. *No kidding.*

Walt was almost licking his lips.

After a few more grueling minutes, the chef pulled out the roasted donut burger and placed it on a plate. He then covered the burger with a thick layer of mustard and ketchup. He placed a leaf of lettuce next to the burger.

When Walt zoomed in on the burger, Ellen finally rolled her eyes. The leaf of lettuce was a contradiction in so many ways.

"There you have it," the chef said, as if he had prepared a masterful meal. "When you try it once, I promise you that you'll want to try it again."

Ellen faced the camera and said with a smile, "We will definitely be trying it, and why don't you come down and try one for yourself? This is Ellen Sheehan for BN-24."

Walt turned off the camera. Ellen turned off her smile.

Before the chef could say something, Ellen walked away. She heard Walt ask if he could try the burger. "Sure," the chef replied with enthusiasm.

Ellen had no desire to watch grown men gorge on something dripping in oil.

She took a deep breath as she stepped outside the restaurant.

She could not do this anymore. She could not cover any more of these kinds of stories. It took a lot of energy on her part to not walk out on the segment, but she had kept thinking of her career.

She now wanted to yell, *What career?!*

She bet Janie did not have to endure what she just had to go through.

Ellen firmly believed she was on par with Janie. In fact, she was better than her.

It was her superiors at BN-24 who did not appreciate her. She wanted to quit and go work for any other station.

But who would hire me? she thought.

Her résumé was not filled with earth-shattering stories. It was filled with the likes of the one she had just covered.

Bridgeton was a big city, and BN-24 was its number one news station. Ellen feared if she walked out, she might end up in a small hick town covering their annual beaver festival.

No. She would not let that happen. She would bite her tongue and do whatever was necessary to stay above her competition. For now, she would do everything Miles and his boss would want from her. The moment she got her chance, though, she would not let it go.

She stuck her hand in her pocket and pulled out a pack of cigarettes. She had quit a few years ago, but the urge to smoke had come back with a vengeance.

She hated herself for craving cigarettes again. It was not that she was overly concerned about her health; she was more concerned for her physical appearance. Her mom used to be a heavy smoker, and she had ended up with lung cancer. But it was the way she looked in those final years that stuck in Ellen's memory. Her mother's face had become etched with deep wrinkles, particularly around her mouth. Her teeth had turned yellowish, and her eyes always had a glazed look.

Ellen put the pack away. She would not mess with the one thing she had going for her: her youthful beauty. She loved being in front of the camera, and she wanted the camera to love her back.

Her shoulders sagged. Right now, she was not feeling any love. Not from the camera, not from her superiors, and not from herself.

She was not sure how many more of these segments she could do.

She took a deep breath and recited her mantra: "You are better than this. You can do this. You can achieve all your goals. No one will give it to you. You have to reach out and take it. Don't worry about the short-term pain, think of the long-term gain. You are Ellen Sheehan. You are a star."

Her cell phone buzzed. She pulled it out of her pocket.

The number was blocked.

She watched as the phone kept ringing.

I should pick it up, she thought. *It can't be worse than the day I'm having.*

"Hello?"

"Is this Ellen Sheehan?" asked a voice. It was heavy and deep, as if someone was purposely altering it.

"Yes. Who is this?"

"My name is not important. What is important is that tomorrow you will get a big surprise. At Chester Station, get on the eight o'clock train going north. I promise you. You will not be disappointed."

Ellen grimaced. "Is this a prank call? If it is, it's not funny."

"It's not," the caller replied. "I saw you on TV. I want to help you."

"Maybe I don't want your help."

"After I hang up, I am going to call Janie Fernandez from SUNTV. I'm sure she'll be interested in what I have to say."

"No, wait!" Ellen yelled. "I'll be there."

"Eight o'clock train, going north," the caller repeated.

He hung up.

Ellen stared at the phone. She was unsure of what to make of it.

Walt came out of the restaurant. "You missed it," he said. "It was the best burger I'd ever eaten."

"Forget about that," Ellen said. "I need you tomorrow at eight o'clock sharp."

"Is it a big story?" he asked.

Ellen nodded. "I have a feeling it will be."

CLOSE YOUR EYES

TWENTY-SIX

Rhodes spent the remainder of the day reading up on Reed Yates's case. His father was correct when he said the police had not gotten far.

Detective Crowder's last entry in the case log book was almost a month old. No wonder Crowder was avoiding Mr. Yates. The detective knew he did not have any answers for him.

Rhodes could not blame Crowder, though.

Investigating a murder was unlike any other job. There were no hard or fast rules, even though most people thought it was an exact science. According to Rhodes, it was more like an art form. Sure, it was the evidence that ultimately defined whether a case was solved or not, but finding that evidence in the first place was the most important part. Sometimes a detective would be inundated with what he believed was vital evidence. That evidence, however, would send him in too many directions at once, wasting valuable time.

Rhodes had come to rely on his intuition. It allowed him to take what was in front of him and pick and choose what was relevant and what was not. It was a way of analyzing risk.

In some ways, an investigation was like peeling an onion. Remove one layer, and another layer would appear underneath. Sometimes a detective would spend days, months, even years removing layers upon layers and end up nowhere.

Rhodes had his share of such cases when he was a detective. He regretted being unable to help solve them. During his time in prison, he would often wonder, *who has taken over my cases? Will he solve them, or will they stay cold?*

He always wished he could use the same investigative techniques that resulted in a conviction, but that was just wishful thinking. Each case came with its own complexities. No two cases were the same. They were each like a giant jigsaw puzzle, and it was his job to put the pieces together. Sometimes the pieces would fit perfectly, and sometimes they would not.

There were many pieces missing in Reed's case. For one thing, something did not seem right. According to his father, Reed was very careful with his belongings, so how did he lose his phone? Sure, he could have forgotten it or even dropped it somewhere, but from the way people described him, he did not come across as someone who was careless. In fact, the cell phone was a gift for his seventeenth birthday. He cherished it so much that he went looking for it, which ultimately led to his death.

Rhodes leaned back and stared at the ceiling. It felt good to be on another investigation. He loved the hunt.

After his conviction, he never imagined he would ever have the opportunity to work on another case. But ever since he got out, they had somehow fallen into his lap.

Tim Yates believed Rhodes could do something to catch his son's killer. Rhodes hoped he would not disappoint him.

TWENTY-SEVEN

Crowder slammed his palm on the counter. "Damn it!"

Normally at this time of the day, the police station's lobby would be swarming with people. Today, however, the place was uncharacteristically empty. There were also no other police officers in sight. The Bridgeton PD had stopped bringing in criminals through the front doors. Handcuffed or not, perps would try to escape the moment they saw an opportunity. They would yell and scream, or sometimes they would try to hurt anyone standing near them. To avoid causing a scene, the BPD started bringing in criminals through the garage doors in the back.

"Take it easy," Officer Shannon said.

Crowder shook his head. "I can't believe they made me give up info on my case."

"Who made you?" Shannon asked.

Crowder scoffed. "The chief. Who else do you think?"

"I bet it was Mr. Yates, right?"

"Yep. His lawyer went straight to the chief and demanded they get an update on the case."

"That's okay," Shannon reassured him. "As the father of the victim, he has a right to know."

"It made me look bad," Crowder complained. "When the chief asked me for a progress report, I had none to give. Plus, I don't even know what Yates would do with that information."

"Don't worry about it. It's not like the chief took the case away from you on his own accord."

"He should have, and told Yates to go solve it himself."

Crowder kept rubbing the wedding ring on his finger.

Shannon leaned back in her chair. "Is this really about the case, or is it more about your marriage?

"Why would you say that? What's wrong with my marriage?"

"For one thing, you cheated on your wife with her co-worker."

"It was a mistake," Crowder replied.

"It always is with you, isn't it?"

"You're not helping."

"What do you want me to say? You messed up and she should forgive you?"

"Yeah, that's what a sensible person would do."

Shannon shook her head. "*Right*," she said sarcastically.

Crowder put his hands over his face. "I miss her."

"Give her time. Right now, the last person she wants to see is you."

"I know, but it's messing me up. It's why I can't seem to close any cases. I can't concentrate. My mind is all over the place."

"How did you meet your wife in the first place?" Shannon asked.

"She rear-ended my BMW. I was ready to give her a piece of my mind, but when I saw her, it was love at first sight. She was smoking hot. I knew I had to marry her."

"If she was so hot, why'd you cheat on her?"

"Unfortunately, her co-worker was even hotter. I couldn't help myself."

Shannon frowned. "Poor you."

"It's my fault, I know. And I take full responsibility for it."

"I'm sure you guys will work it out."

"What if we don't?"

"You guys don't have any kids, so I don't see a problem for both of you to move on. By the way, where are you sleeping right now?"

Crowder leaned in and whispered, "I'll tell you if you promise not to tell anyone."

"Okay, sure."

"I'm sleeping in my BMW."

"What?!" Shannon replied a little too loudly.

Crowder looked around in case anyone heard her. Then he whispered, "I'm still paying rent for the condo my wife is living in, and my child support payments are taking a chunk out of my salary, so I can't rent a place right now."

"Is that why you want to get back together? Because you can't afford another divorce?"

Crowder sighed. "Yeah, that too. But I do still love her."

Shannon shook her head. "You have an odd way of showing love to the women you marry, you know that?"

TWENTY-EIGHT

She was a heavyset woman with a thick European accent. She wore a big sweater, even though the weather was mild outside. Her short blonde hair was tied in a ponytail.

Rhodes was in the basement of a two-story house. He had found the rental in the classified section of the local newspaper.

The landlady's name was Olya. She did not give her last name. Rhodes did not care whether he knew her full name or not. The only thing that mattered was that the price was right.

"There is hot water," Olya said, turning on the kitchen tap. "There is heating, but no central air conditioning. You can buy your own unit, but it's usually cool in the basement during the summer, so you won't need it. Plus, if you put one in and keep it on all the time, my electric bill will go up. I don't want to raise your rent, you understand?"

Rhodes nodded.

The basement apartment had one bedroom, an open space in the living room, a tiny kitchen, and a washroom. The ceilings were just high enough for Rhodes to avoid bumping his head. There were two windows—one in the bedroom and another in the living room. The entrance to the basement was through a narrow door at the back of the house.

All in all, the space was small for a man his size. But Rhodes could not complain. He had lived in a space smaller than this for ten years, after all. Plus, the apartment would only be temporary. Once he found stable employment, Rhodes would find a better home.

Olya said, "The laundromat is down the street. It is open twenty-four hours. Do you smoke?"

Rhodes shook his head.

"You have any pets?"

Rhodes shook his head.

"You went to jail?" she asked.

He nodded.

She did not seem too surprised or shocked by his answer. Maybe she was used to renting to tenants with criminal records. "The rent is four-fifty a month. You have to pay first and last to start, and all in cash. I don't take checks. The previous tenant ran away without paying his rent. He was a student and was really nice. He made me agree to take checks. His first couple of months were okay, but then his last check bounced. I asked him to pay me in cash, but then he just disappeared one night. He left all this stuff behind."

Rhodes had noticed a small table and two chairs that were used for dining. There was a mattress and a box in the bedroom. A stained sofa was in the living room, but there was no TV or microwave. Olya had assured him that the stove worked, though.

"If you want to rent, you can use the furniture," she said. "I have a bad back. I don't want to throw this stuff out unless you want to buy it and move it someplace else?"

Rhodes shook his head.

"I live on the main floor," Olya continued. "The top unit is rented to a single mother and her daughter. The mother smokes, but she does it outside. The daughter is a teenager, and I sometimes see her walking back from school. I see a guy come and go, but I didn't ask if it's the mother's boyfriend or the girl's father. It's none of my business, you know. If they keep paying their rent on time, I have no problem with what they do. Are you single?"

Rhodes nodded.

"Okay, but no wild parties. The student used to bring his girlfriend over all the time. And when his friends would come over, it would get loud and noisy. There were many times I had to come downstairs in the middle of the night and tell him to turn the music down. Oh, the music!" She shivered. "I didn't understand it. It was all boom-boom-boom."

Rhodes assumed she was mimicking the bass of the sound.

"So, do you want it or not?" Olya asked. "I got more people interested in renting it. Decide quickly, because this place will be off the market very soon."

Rhodes doubted that. From the state of the apartment, it looked like it had not been occupied for at least a month.

There were other places he still wanted to check out. They were nicer than this place, but he feared the landlords would be hesitant to rent to an ex-con. Plus, the price for the basement apartment was the lowest he could find.

"I'll take it," he said.

She smiled. "Great. When do you want to move in?"

"Right now."

"Where is your stuff?" she asked.
Rhodes held up his duffel bag. "It's all here."

TWENTY-NINE

Ellen looked at her watch. It was ten minutes to eight. She was on the platform of Chester Station. Walt was standing next to her, carrying his video camera. A BTA employee stood next to Walt. He was in charge of taking care of the BN-24 crew.

When Ellen had received the anonymous phone call, the first thing she did was contact BTA. She told them she wanted to do a segment on the outdated transit equipment and how it was affecting the riders. She sealed the deal when she told them her focus was to encourage politicians to invest more in public transit. She could not tell them the real reason she was there. In fact, even she was not sure what this was all about. But she had to take a chance. She would be foolish not to. Dan Ferguson had already hijacked her story, and she sure as hell would not let him hijack another one.

What Miles did was unforgivable. She wanted to argue that his action could be construed as sexist, but she knew that would not stick because it was Miles's boss who called the shots at BN-24—and his boss was a woman.

Ellen had to pick her battles carefully. She could not start something and then have it come back and bite her.

A train entered the terminal and came to a halt.

Ellen checked her watch. The caller had said the eight o'clock train. This one was early.

The doors opened. Walt moved towards the train. Ellen stopped him. "We'll take the next one."

"Why?" he asked, looking irritated. "We've already seen three go by."

She glared at him. "I said we'll take the next one."

He shrugged. "Okay, sure. You're the boss."

The doors closed and the train moved out of the station.

Ellen began to sweat underneath her green suit. She hoped her makeup was still okay. She wanted to look good for her big shot. She adjusted her suit jacket and her sleeves in order to let cool air seep into her body.

She looked at her watch again. Two minutes to go before eight. Time was crawling at a snail's pace.

She looked over at the BTA employee. He was busy smiling at passengers standing on the platform. He was probably happy to help a news crew. Maybe he would get a chance to be on TV.

Ellen was not sure if she would ask him any questions. *Maybe I should*, she thought. *It might make my cover feel more real.* Plus, if all this was a sick joke, then it was better to make nice with the BTA folks. In her profession, connections meant a great deal. If this all went south, then the people at BTA might not give her access to BTA's facilities in the future. They might even give exclusive access only to SUNTV—and Janie Fernandez.

Ellen gritted her teeth. There was no way she would lose to her.

Another train entered the station. Ellen turned to Walt. "Get your camera ready."

Walt lifted the heavy camera to his shoulder.

The train's doors opened.

Ellen, Walt, and the BTA employee boarded. They moved to the middle of the compartment. Ellen scanned the interior. Rush-hour commuters were piling aboard. She spotted a man in a suit. She went up to him and introduced herself.

"Do you mind if I asked you a few questions?" she said.

The man adjusted his tie, smiled, and nodded. He quickly patted down his hair.

"What's your name?" Ellen quickly asked.

"Paul."

"Do you take the train regularly?"

"Every day."

"Good." Ellen pulled out a microphone from her purse and steadied herself.

Walt gave her a thumbs-up. When the camera's red light came on, she said, "This is Ellen Sheehan from BN-24. I am on a Bridgeton Transit Authority subway train, and with me here is Paul. Paul is a regular BTA rider. He takes the train every day to work. Now Paul, what has been your experience using the public transit system?"

She pushed the microphone closer to him. He cleared his throat and said, "Some days it's fine, and I get to work on time, but there are times where there are track problems, or signal problems, or the train ahead of us is having mechanical problems."

Ellen said, "Does this mean you are late for work?"

He nodded. "Yes."

"A lot?"

He hesitated. "Enough times."

"And what does your boss say?"

"He doesn't give me a hard time. He knows how often the system breaks down."

Ellen smiled and turned to the camera. "Well, there you have it, folks. Our transit system is so bad that even Paul's boss has come to accept the problem. Unfortunately, not all bosses can be like Paul's. We'll talk to more passengers and find out how they cope with the system. This is Ellen Sheehan for BN-24."

The red light went off. Ellen stopped smiling.

"Was that okay?" Paul asked, concerned about his performance.

"Yeah, yeah, it's fine," Ellen said, waving him off.

Walt gave Paul a thumbs-up.

Ellen looked at her watch again. It was fifteen after eight.

Ellen eyed the passengers on the train. She was not sure what she was looking for, but something told her it had to do with them.

"Do you want to interview anyone else?" Walt asked.

"Yes, but let's go to the next car." Ellen turned to the BTA employee, who was standing by dutifully.

"Sure," he said, looking eager to help.

They went into the next car. Ellen eyed the passengers, but then she decided to go to the next car.

They moved from car to car. At each station, passengers boarded and disembarked in a steady cycle. To avoid arousing suspicion, Ellen would stop a rider and ask them about their experiences with the transit system. What did they like or dislike? What did they believe BTA could improve upon? Were they satisfied with any changes BTA had tried to implement?

In between her interviews, Ellen kept surveying the people around her.

When they were almost at the end of the train, Ellen had a sinking feeling that someone had played a sick joke on her. *Maybe Janie put me up to this*, she thought. *God, I hate her even more now.*

She could not believe she was fooled into thinking she would find something. At least she had covered herself. The interviews on the train would support her reason for being there.

Then she spotted a peculiar looking passenger. He was sitting on the seat across from her, and he had his head tilted to the side. Ellen could not tell if he was breathing or not.

Ellen moved closer to him.

She was inches from his face when he suddenly awoke with a start. "Uh, what…?" he said, looking around.

"I'm so sorry," Ellen said. "I thought you weren't…"

"I was sleeping," he quickly said. "Can't a man take a nap in peace?"

Walt and the BTA employee exchanged glances. They were probably wondering if she had lost her mind.

Ellen walked away from the passenger.

She began to sweat. Her body felt like it was in a sauna. She wanted to pull off her jacket and get off the train at the next stop.

A woman screamed. Ellen looked up. On the other side of the compartment, a woman was standing with her hand over her mouth.

Ellen rushed up to her.

"What's wrong?" she demanded.

Without saying a word, the lady pointed at a woman in a wheelchair. She wore a dark sweater, sunglasses, and had long hair. She was sitting with her head tilted back.

Ellen was not sure why the other woman had screamed, but when she looked carefully, she realized something was wrong.

She moved in closer.

There were deep sockets beneath the sunglasses as if someone had scooped out the woman's eyes.

Ellen had to cover her mouth to stop herself from screaming.

THIRTY

Jo headed to the scene the moment she got the call. She raced down the steps, and when she reached the platform, she found Walters and Chief Baker locked in a heated argument.

"It's our case," Baker said. "Detective Crowder will take over the investigation."

Jo spotted Crowder in the corner. He was staring at his cell phone. He looked like he had other things on his mind than the dead body found on the train.

Walters replied, "It's the same MO. We are dealing with the same killer."

"I let the FBI have the first one, but this one belongs to the Bridgeton Police," Baker said.

"It's not about who gets the credit…"

"It always is, isn't it?" he shot back.

Walters composed her feelings. "We are already working on a subway murder case. It doesn't make sense for you to be working on one too."

"What if it's not the same person?" Baker asked.

It was Walters's turn to raise her voice. "You really think random people are dropping off dead bodies on trains? Do you really?"

"I never said that," Baker claimed. "All I'm saying is there might be a possibility that the two cases are not connected."

"Well, they are. A serial killer is using the subway to dispose of his victims."

The mere mention of a serial killer gave Baker pause.

The Special Agent in Charge and the Chief of Police stared at each other.

"We're a federal agency. We can supersede your authority," Walters said.

Baker's eyes narrowed. "We got the nine-one-one call, so it's ours. If I have to bring the mayor into this, I will."

"We already have our people on site. Plus, by standing here arguing, we are delaying the BTA's operations."

"I don't care. I already caved once. I'm not letting this one go."

Jo shook her head. Her boss and Baker were both going through a power trip. She walked over to them and said, "Why don't the FBI and the Bridgeton PD work together on this one?"

"What?" Walters and Baker asked in unison.

"Yes," Jo said. "We haven't been able to make much progress on the first victim, so it might be better if we combined our resources."

Under normal circumstances, Jo would have preferred to work alone. She believed if another person joined her, it would only slow her down. Plus, she was well aware of Crowder's reputation for womanizing and hardheadedness. She did not want to waste time and energy butting heads with him. But she knew if the case ended up in the BPD's hands, it might complicate her own investigation. There was a killer on the loose who was playing an evil game. Jo did not want jurisdictional pettiness to get in the way of stopping him.

Baker and Walters did not look convinced.

"Look," Jo said, "we're wasting valuable time here. If we keep finding more dead bodies, believe me, it won't look good for the bureau or the BPD."

Walters said, "Okay, I'll go with it, but the FBI will run the operation. Your detective can join us. Whatever we do, we'll do it together."

Baker mulled this over. He knew if he did not agree, there would be a stalemate. Plus, it would be good to get Crowder away from the station. Baker knew he had been going through some personal issues. Quite frankly, the man was in a funk. This might do both the department and him some good.

"Alright. But when there is an arrest, the Bridgeton PD will also get the credit."

"Agreed," Walters said.

Baker waved Crowder over. Crowder slipped the phone in his pocket and strolled over to them.

"Detective Crowder," Baker said. "I'm sure you've met Agent Pullinger before."

"I have," Crowder replied. "Agent Pullinger has taken quite of a few of my cases."

Great beginning, Jo thought.

The truth was that Jo had indeed taken over Crowder's cases, though she would insist that she did not take them by choice. They were handed to her because the Bureau felt it was in their best interest to focus on those cases.

Baker said, "She'll be your new partner in this investigation. I'm sure both of you will get along nicely."

"I'm sure," Crowder said.

Walters said, "Ben is already in there. You might want to check out the body."

Jo looked over at Crowder. He gestured towards the train. "Ladies first."

Jo entered the train. She quickly spotted Ben. He was examining a body in a wheelchair.

"I thought that would never end," Ben said, looking up at her. She knew he meant the catfight between Walters and Baker.

"Detective Crowder will be working on the case as well," Jo said.

"Detective," Ben said, nodding in his direction.

Crowder nodded back.

"So, what have you found?" Jo asked.

"Not much, I'm afraid, except that she was mutilated by having her eyes gouged out. And by the looks of it, the killer used a crude object."

"Do you know who she is?" Jo asked.

"There is no ID on her person, but I've taken her fingerprints. If she's in our database, we'll know who she is."

Crowder leaned down and examined the victim's face. There were hollow circles where the eyes should have been. Crowder's mouth contorted in disgust as he moved away from the body.

"Is there any writing?" Jo said.

"What writing?" Crowder asked.

"The first victim had a message carved on his chest. If it's the same killer, I'll bet there is a message on her."

"Let's find out," Ben said.

He examined her arms and legs by lifting her sleeves. He peeked through her shirt collar and said, "Nothing on the chest. Maybe it's on the back." He pushed the body forward and pulled the shirt up.

"I see something," Ben said.

Jo moved behind the wheelchair to get a better view.

Scrawled on her skin were the words: WHAT THE EYES SEE.

"What does that mean?" Crowder asked.

"I don't know," Jo replied. "But whoever is doing this, he is leaving messages for *us*."

THIRTY-ONE

Jo left the subway car and found Walters in a heated confrontation with a woman. Jo recognized her when she got closer. It was Ellen Sheehan. Jo had a few run-ins with her before. In Jo's opinion, Sheehan was trying too hard to be taken seriously. This meant sometimes she could be a bit too aggressive in her pursuit of a story.

"How did you know there would be a body on that train?" Walters asked.

"I didn't."

"The BTA employee told us that you were constantly looking at your watch."

"I'm on a tight schedule. I wanted to make sure we had enough footage for the evening news."

Walters narrowed her eyes. "I find it highly suspicious that you and your cameraman happened to be on the same train where another body was discovered."

"I don't know what to tell you," Sheehan claimed.

"Why don't you just tell us the truth?"

"I told you, I was there to cover the public transit system. I interviewed riders on the train. You can talk to Walt, my cameraman. He'll back me up. In fact, we have the footage to prove it."

"Do you also have footage of the victim?" Walters asked.

Sheehan opened her mouth and then shut it.

"Because if you do," Walters continued, "we want a copy of it."

Sheehan crossed her arms. "You'll need a warrant to see it."

Walters glared at her.

Sheehan said, "I'll let you have it, but under one condition: you let me interview you."

"Why would we do that when we can just confiscate the video?"

"On what basis?" Sheehan replied.

"Evidence that could be crucial in a murder investigation."

It was Sheehan's turn to glare at her.

Jo spotted Dennis Wilmont on the platform. He waved her over.

"Agent Pullinger, right?" he said.

"That's right."

"The moment I heard about the second body, I got my guys working on it right away. Come, I'll show you something."

Jo said, "Detective Jay Crowder is also working on the case. Whatever you have to show me, you can show him as well."

"Okay, sure."

Crowder joined them in the station's security office. Inside, a transit officer was working behind a large monitor.

"Run the tape," Wilmont said to him.

On the screen, they saw an empty subway platform.

"What station is that?" Jo asked.

"It was taken at Sherbourne Station," the officer replied.

"And that is…?"

"Ten stations down on the southbound line."

"Okay."

They stared at the vacant platform. Suddenly, a man appeared from behind a pillar. He was wearing a checkered shirt, black pants, and a baseball cap. The man was pushing a woman in a wheelchair. It was the victim.

The man stopped at the edge of the platform. He did not look up. Nor did he look left or right. He just stared at the tracks. More passengers appeared on the platform, but no one noticed him. Why would they? They probably thought he was with his mother or another relative.

The train appeared on the screen and halted at the station. The doors opened, and the man wheeled the woman in the wheelchair inside the train.

The doors closed and the train pulled out of the terminal.

"Do you know where he got off?" Jo asked.

The officer fast-forwarded the video. He then played it at a normal speed. The next image was another platform. There were people already waiting for the train.

"What station is that?" Jo asked.

"Chester Station."

Jo squinted. In the middle of the platform, she spotted Ellen Sheehan, her cameraman, and a BTA officer.

The officer was right. Sheehan was constantly looking at her watch, as if she was waiting for something to happen. But the video was not enough to prove anything.

The train pulled into the station, and the doors opened.

Jo watched as Sheehan, the cameraman, and the BTA officer entered the train.

Just then, at the bottom of the screen, the man with the baseball cap left the train from another car. He had his hands in his pockets as he walked out of view.

The transit officer typed on his keyboard and the image flipped on the monitor. The man took the escalators up and then walked through the turnstiles and out of the station.

The man never once looked up.

He knew where the security cameras were, Jo thought.

THIRTY-TWO

Rhodes gripped the steering wheel firmly as he pressed on the accelerator. Even though he hadn't driven a car in over ten years, there were some things a person never forgot. The twenty-year-old Chevy Malibu felt good under his control. It had taken a few kicks to get it started, and the engine was a bit too loud, but for five hundred dollars, Rhodes could not complain.

The salesman at the dealership had told him the three hundred thousand miles on the odometer was nothing to be concerned about. The black beauty, as he liked to call it, would give another three hundred thousand if Rhodes took care of it.

Rhodes doubted very much if the car gave him even fifty thousand miles, but he was not planning on driving it for long. Right now, it was more of a means to an end. Just as long as it got him from point A to point B without any trouble, Rhodes would be satisfied.

It had started to drizzle. The rubber on the windshield wipers had worn out, but they were still enough to clear his view.

Rhodes turned on the heater. The salesperson had already told him the air conditioning did not work, so Rhodes did not bother checking it. If the car made it to summer, Rhodes would roll down the windows.

He was pulling the car into the back of the house when he spotted someone wearing baggy clothes and a hoodie sitting on the steps of his basement apartment.

He parked the car and waited. He hoped the noise of the engine would make the person turn toward him.

He then saw the person was also wearing big headphones.

Rhodes grunted.

He honked.

The person did not turn.

He honked again, this time letting it run longer.

The person got up and turned.

It was a girl.

She wore baggy clothes. She had on dark mascara, dark lipstick, and she had a tomboy haircut

"Sorry, I didn't know you were back," she said as Rhodes got out of the car.

"Who are you?" he asked.

"I live on the second floor with my mom."

Rhodes looked around. "Why are you out in the rain?"

"My mom isn't back from work yet."

"You don't have a key?"

"She doesn't trust me."

"Why don't you go to a coffee shop or a friend's house?"

"I don't have any money, and my friends live a bit far."

"You shouldn't be outside. You might catch a cold."

He was not sure why he was concerned. He did not know her, and it was none of his business what she did.

"Is it okay if I just sit here? It's better than sitting on my steps."

Rhodes looked up at the sky. The clouds had gotten darker. The drizzle would soon turn to heavy rain.

"How old are you?" he asked.

"Fifteen."

Rhodes would have invited her inside, but as a former cop, he knew it would not look good for a fifteen-year-old to be hanging around a man his age.

"You can wait for your mom in my car," he said.

He let her in and then went inside his apartment.

He had picked up a few groceries while on his way home. He went into the kitchen and fried himself a couple of sausages. He applied some butter to his toast and then pulled out a bottle of beer from a twelve-pack.

The rain had started to come down heavy. He glanced out the window. He could see the girl in the passenger seat of his car.

What if I hadn't come home early? he thought. *She'd be soaked by now.*

He sat down at the table and ate his meal in silence.

Half an hour later, the rain had cleared out. He went to the window and spotted a woman approaching the house. She disappeared from view.

Rhodes put the dishes in the sink and went outside.

He was about to open the car door when he stopped. The girl was curled up on the seat. Her arms were wrapped around her knees and she was fast asleep.

She is just a kid, he thought.

He went back inside.

The next time he came out to check on her, she was gone.

THIRTY-THREE

Jo found Chris sitting behind his laptop, watching a movie.

"Is that what you do at work?" Jo said.

Chris was not fazed. He just pointed to a triangular sign on top of his cubicle. It read *DO NOT DISTURB, ON BREAK*.

"Flip it," he said.

She did. There was another sign underneath it: *DO NOT DISTURB, NAPPING*.

"Flip it one more time," he said with a smile.

Jo did. The last sign read *IF YOU ARE HOT (IRINA), PLEASE DO DISTURB*.

"Has Irina seen this?" Jo asked.

"Yep, and she ripped it up. But I always print more."

Chris finally noticed the man standing next to Jo. "Can I help you?"

Jo said, "This is Detective Jay Crowder from the Bridgeton PD. He'll be working with us on the case."

"Hey, I didn't know," Chris said.

Crowder shrugged.

Jo dropped a DVD on Chris's desk. "This is from BTA's CCTV cameras. I doubt we'll find anything, but find out whatever you can."

"Will do."

Chris turned back to his movie.

Jo stared at him.

"I'm on break, remember," he said.

She left him and took Crowder over to her desk.

He took a seat across from her and smirked. "Nice office you guys got here. I had thought about becoming a Fed too, but I didn't want to go through the academy. Too much work."

Jo was not in the mood for small talk. Crowder was here to assist the FBI in apprehending a serial killer. The sooner they captured the killer, the sooner this arrangement could come to an end.

She said, "What do you think of the case?"

On the drive over to the field office, Jo had given a copy of the case files to Crowder to read. She wanted him caught up.

"I think we need to focus on the message the killer left on the victims' bodies," he said.

Jo flipped open the file on her desk and retrieved a photo of the carving on the first victim. "What the hands touch," she said. She then pulled out her phone and scrolled through the images until she found the one she took of the second victim. "What the eyes see."

"Right," Crowder said. "The first victim's hands were removed, which was referenced with a message on his body. The second victim's eyes were removed. This was referenced with a message on her body. Maybe someone did something to the killer and he is punishing them for it."

Jo thought about it. "You think his victims had hurt him?"

Crowder shrugged. "I don't know, maybe. But what we do know is that most serial killers are usually acting out their deranged fantasies, or they reenact what they perceive as injustices done to them in childhood. For instance, if girls ignored or spurned them when they were young, as adults, they would try to correct this by overpowering women with the aim of controlling them."

Jo stared at him. "That's a good observation."

Crowder grinned. "I'm not all eye candy, you know."

Tarik came over. "So I checked out Sherbourne Station, and just like the last time, we don't have a clear shot of the killer. There is a parking lot across from the station entrance. A camera caught the killer exiting the doors and then walking down the street. He then disappeared around the corner. The next thing I saw was a Mercedes-Benz driving away. It was a side view, so I could not get the license plate number. But I bet it's the same car the killer used the last time." Tarik held up a DVD. "I got a copy from the parking lot if you want to see it."

"I don't think we'll find anything," Jo said. "The killer knows exactly what he's doing. In the subway stations, he never once looks up at the cameras. And when he leaves, he knows where to park his car so that no camera captures his plate number. Oh, by the way, this is Detective Jay Crowder. He's working on the case with us."

Tarik shook his hand. "I heard Walters mention something. Welcome aboard."

Jo leaned back in her chair. "What I don't understand is, we have footage of him exiting the stations, but we don't have any footage of him entering the subway. How is that possible?"

Tarik said, "If I remember correctly, there are almost forty subway stations, I'm sure he slipped in through one of them. We could ask BTA for all their security footage for the last week."

"We would need extra resources to comb through that much data."

"Chris could do it," Tarik said.

"Chris can try, but he is just one person. Plus, if the killer is that careful in his getaway, I'm sure he is even more careful when he is dropping off his victims."

Crowder chimed in. "From what you guys just told me, he uses the Mercedes to escape. What if he uses another vehicle for the drop off?"

They were silent for a moment. They were all thinking the same thing: *What if there are not one, but two people involved in this?*

Irina came over. "The victim's name is Natasha Wedham. She lives with her boyfriend on the east side of the city."

Crowder jumped up from his chair and said, "I'm Detective Jay Crowder from the Bridgeton PD. I'm also working on the case. You must be Irina."

Crowder held out his hand. Irina reluctantly shook it.

Crowder gave her his best smile. "Your co-worker was right. You are hot."

Irina looked at Jo as if to get her permission to clock Crowder.

Jo said, "Do you have an address?"

"Right here," Irina replied, dropping a piece of paper on her desk.

Jo grabbed it and said, "Let's go, Detective Crowder. We've got work to do." Jo wanted to get Crowder out of the office before any blood was spilled.

THIRTY-FOUR

Rhodes slowed the Malibu as he passed by a pizza shop's parking lot. According to the report, it was in this parking lot that Reed Yates was shot.

The area was known for gang-related crimes, and as such, police presence was all around. Rhodes had counted four cruisers on his way to the shop. This also meant that Rhodes could not sit in the Malibu and keep an eye on the place. He would easily be mistaken for an undercover cop.

He turned the car around and pulled into a strip mall. He parked the car and got out. He decided to go to a bagel shop.

He ordered a sandwich and coffee and found a seat by the windows. He was half a block away from the pizza shop, but he had a clear view of it from where he was seated.

Rhodes ate slowly. He chewed each bite and took small sips.

It did not take long for him to realize something else was going on.

A car pulled into the shop's parking lot and stopped. Two seconds later, a kid, no older than thirteen, ran out from the side of the shop and up to the car. The kid exchanged a few words with the driver, shook his hand, and then ran into the pizza shop. He came back out, shook hands once again with the driver, and disappeared around the side of the shop. The car then drove away. All this happened in less than a minute.

To an untrained eye, nothing looked out of the ordinary, but Rhodes knew what had just happened: a drug exchange.

By the time Rhodes had finished his meal, he had seen four exchanges occur.

The pizza shop was used as a drug depot. This meant where there was lots of cash. So, there was always security, specifically, cameras.

Rhodes was certain one of them had caught Reed's shooting.

The owner of the shop had told Crowder the shop's security cameras were not working. In his report, Crowder had stated he had confirmed this by examining the equipment, but Rhodes was certain that was only half the story. The owner had shown Crowder only what he needed to see. Rhodes was certain there was fully functioning equipment in the back that had captured what had transpired outside the shop.

The only way to find out was to do something.

Rhodes left the bagel shop, drove up to the pizzeria, and stopped the Malibu in front of it. He checked the side-view mirror and spotted the boy coming toward him.

The boy stopped by the driver's side window.

Rhodes had folded a twenty dollar bill in his palm. He held his hand out for the boy, but instead of taking it, the boy said, "What'd you want?"

"I need a score," Rhodes said nonchalantly.

The boy scrunched up his face. "I don't know what you're talking about?"

"Someone told me I can buy some goods here."

"They told you wrong, man."

"You don't work in the pizza shop?"

"I do."

"Then why did you run up to my car?"

"I'm like the guy at a drive-thru. What kind of pizza do you want?" he asked.

The boy was sharp, Rhodes could tell. Someone must have trained him well. There was no way he was taking orders for slices of pizza. Rhodes had never once seen the boy return to a car with a pizza box or a paper bag. He always came out, concealing something in his hand.

"Come on," Rhodes said. "I drove all the way here because someone told me you guys have the best goods."

"Listen, I don't know what you are talking about, man. You're a cop or something?"

Rhodes wanted to tell him he was actually a convicted felon, but he knew the boy or even his boss would not believe him. Rhodes still had the demeanor of a police officer. Even after ten years behind bars, he reeked of detective.

"We don't like the police, you get me?" the boy said and walked away.

Rhodes cursed.

He put the car in gear and drove away.

THIRTY-FIVE

The room was dark and closed off from the outside world. There were no windows and just one door. The walls were dirty and grimy. The floor was wet and sticky. The fluorescent tube light flickered constantly.

None of this bothered Jacopo.

He was seated at a table. His tools were spread before him. He picked up a corrugated saw and examined it. There was rust on the blade, but he was not too concerned. The longer it took to get the job done, the more pain his victims endured.

He never imagined he was capable of inflicting so much hurt on another human being. But now he realized he actually enjoyed it. Maybe it had to do with the hurt he felt inside him. When he tortured someone, he was actually releasing his suffering. The entire process was, in some ways, cathartic. When he was done torturing a victim, he always felt like a new person.

He put the saw down and lifted a scalpel. It, too, was rusted.

The walls vibrated, and he heard the sounds of metal on metal. A train passed through a tunnel adjacent to the room. He placed his hand over the tools to stop them from falling off the table.

Within seconds, the sound had subsided. He went back to examining his tools.

The room was filthy and depressing compared to his current accommodations. But he would never dare say this to his master. After all, it was his master who had given him a new life.

His real name was Craig Orton. He was once married. He also had a child. He used to work for a mining company, but after years of spending time underground, he developed a lung disease. His company quickly released him when they found out his condition. He got a lawyer and tried to sue them, but they had lawyers too, and theirs were more effective than his. His savings dried up, and he became an alcoholic. His marriage fell apart, and his wife took his daughter away from him. It did not help that he had become abusive toward his wife. But she did not understand what he was going through. The company he had worked day and night for had robbed him of a future.

He drifted from shelter to shelter until he ended up on the streets. His condition worsened, and he was good as dead when a man approached him one night. The man stayed in the shadows, but he offered Craig a chance at a new life.

The man put him in a private health facility where doctors monitored him twenty-four-seven. They gave him powerful medication that destroyed whatever disease had infected his lungs. Three months later, he was cured.

The man reappeared again, and he gave him a brand new car and an apartment in a nice part of the city. The man told him he would take care of him, but he had to do whatever the man asked of him, even if it meant killing and torturing another person.

He never hesitated for one minute in following the man's commands. It was a small price to pay for what the man had done for him.

The man then gave him the name *Jacopo*. The man also told him he was going to be his master, and Jacopo was going to be his student.

He accepted this without question. After all, it was his master who had given him life, and in return, he would take a life for him.

There was something else that propelled him to do what was asked of him. He feared his master. His master had a plan, and Jacopo knew if he did not follow through with it, his master would make him suffer a fate far worse than what he made his victims suffer.

He shivered at that thought.

He knew soon enough his master would reappear with another task for him.

Jacopo went back to his tools. He wanted to be ready for when it happened.

THIRTY-SIX

Rhodes sat on the sofa with Reed's file spread out next to him. For the last couple of hours, he had pondered ways to get inside the pizza shop. He could not ask the local police for help. He knew once Detective Crowder found out an outsider was working on his case, he would make Rhodes's life even more difficult.

He could make another attempt and hope a different boy was running the drugs. But this came with a huge risk. If he got caught, there was no telling what the gang would do to him once they found out he was *not* a narc officer. Rhodes had no interest in finding out.

There had to be another way.

There was a knock at the door. Rhodes's back tensed. No one knew his address. *Who could that be?* he thought.

There was another knock.

Rhodes looked around the apartment, but there was nothing he could use as a weapon.

He slowly moved to the door and without opening it, he said, "Who is it?"

"It's Tess," a female voice said from the other side.

"Who?"

"I live on the top floor."

Rhodes relaxed. It was the girl he had found sitting on his front steps.

He opened the door. The girl was dressed like the day before, but this time her mascara was all over her face. She looked like she had been crying.

"Can I sit in your car?"

"Why?"

"I had a fight with my mom, and I need a place to stay."

Rhodes did not want to get involved. It was none of his business. He had a lot on his plate as it was. He knew he should tell her to go away or shut the door on her. But he knew he would not. He had a soft spot for those in need.

In fact, that was what got him sent to prison in the first place.

Ten years ago, a woman came to him for help. Her child had been murdered, and she believed it was the boy's father. No one believed her. The boy's father was a respectable member of society. She was an addict and known to the police. Rhodes should have sent her away. But he felt pity for her. She was weak, and society had failed her. But he would not.

Rhodes never regretted taking on her case, but he did regret what he did at the end of it.

Rhodes sighed. He went out and unlocked the Malibu's doors.

"Thanks," Tess said as she got in.

Rhodes went back inside.

A few hours later, Rhodes was exhausted from looking over the file. He needed fresh air. He decided to go for a drive. It would help clear his head and his mind. Maybe once he returned, he would find a way into the pizza shop.

He grabbed his coat and put his hands in his pockets. One of his hands felt a card. He pulled it out. It was the one given to him by Barry Kowalski at the bar.

Rhodes gritted his teeth. He knew that sooner or later, he would have to deal with his father.

He might as well do it now.

He went out and found the car empty.

The girl must have left. I hope she has sorted out her problems with her mom.

He started the engine and drove away.

Wilmington was a two-hour drive from Bridgeton. The last time Rhodes was there was over twenty years ago. He had promised himself he would never go back. The city brought back bad memories. And all those memories involved his father.

He had driven for an hour when he heard a loud noise. He looked around. He was sure he had not hit anything.

He heard the noise again.

Do I have a flat tire? He wondered.

He parked the car by the side of the road and got out. There was nothing around him except for trees and bushes. The nearest gas station was about a mile away. If he had a flat, he would have to change it himself.

He checked each tire and found all four were inflated.

What the hell? Well, the car's so old, maybe it is acting up.

He heard the noise again and realized it was not car-related. It was something else.

He moved to the back of the car. The noise was coming from the trunk.

He popped it open and moved back, expecting something to jump at him. Instead, he saw the girl curled up inside. She squinted as the light hit her face.

"What're you doing in there?" he asked, surprised.

"I was sleeping."

His brow furrowed in puzzlement. "Why in the trunk?"

She did not answer him. Instead, she pulled herself out and patted her jacket and jeans. "You should clean it. It's so dirty in there."

Rhodes felt anger rise in him. "It's not made for sleeping," he growled. Then something occurred to him. "How did you get in the trunk?" Rhodes had the keys on him the entire time.

"Through the back seat."

Tess gestured to the back seats. Rhodes saw the trunk was accessible from the inside once the seats were pulled down.

"Why were you in the trunk?" Rhodes asked.

She looked away.

"I'm asking you a question."

She shook her head and bit her bottom lip. "I was trying to hide, okay?"

Rhodes's eyes narrowed. "From who?"

"My mom's boyfriend. He's a creep. He's tried to hit on me. I've told my mom many times, but she won't believe me."

"Is that why you had a fight with your mom?"

"Yeah."

Rhodes put his hands in his pockets and stepped away from her. He needed to think. *If the girl is missing, will the mother call the police on me?* He had not kidnapped her. She had snuck in without his knowledge. But when pressed, would she give that statement? She was only fifteen, and kids that age would do anything, even lie, to avoid getting in trouble.

"Can I come with you?" she asked.

"No."

"Why not?"

"You're not supposed to be getting in cars with strangers."

"But you're not a stranger. You live in the same house as me."

"Yeah, but I have a lot of work to do, and I can't babysit you."

"So, are you going to leave me here alone?"

Rhodes looked around. The last town was a couple of miles away. He sighed. "Fine. Get in."

"As I said, my name is Tess," she said, strapping herself in the passenger seat. "Tess Connelly."

Rhodes put the car in gear.

"What's your name?" she asked.

Rhodes did not respond.

"I told you mine. You have to tell me yours."

"If I tell you, will you be quiet for the rest of the drive?"

"Okay, I guess."

"It's Martin," he replied. "Martin Rhodes."

Rhodes was not in any mood for chit-chat. He never was. Right now, though, he had a bigger problem waiting for him in Wilmington.

THIRTY-SEVEN

They were in a two-bedroom bungalow on the west side of the city. The living room was decorated with antique furniture.

Jo and Crowder sat across from Jeremy Turnbull. Jeremy's long, thinning hair was combed back. He had stubble on his face, and he had a large tattoo on his right arm.

Jeremy was Natasha Wedham's boyfriend.

"How can someone do such a thing?" he asked the two detectives.

Jo had heard that question many times before, and each time, she found herself wondering the same thing: *How can someone take another person's life?* Birth was beautiful and filled with endless opportunities. Death was ugly, and there was no return from it.

"What can you tell us about Natasha?" Jo asked.

"She was smart, funny, and I loved her."

"What did Natasha do for a living?"

"She worked as a nurse at a retirement home."

"What did she do before that?"

He shrugged. "I don't know. She mentioned something about working with the mentally ill."

"When did she go missing?" Jo asked.

"Yesterday," he replied. "She never came home after work, and I thought maybe she was working a long shift. It's happened before when someone becomes severely ill, or when someone dies and they need extra staff to console the other residents. I finally called her cell phone, and there was no answer. I then called the retirement home, and they said she'd left hours ago. I got worried and called all our family and friends, but no one had heard from her. I then went to the police. They said they would have to wait twenty-four hours before they could open a missing persons case. By the time the twenty-four hours were up, you guys called and..."

He took a deep breath.

Men were different than women, Jo knew. They felt it was a weakness if they cried in front of strangers. At a time like this, it did not matter if you were male or female. Mourning was a natural part of the grieving process.

"What do you do?" she asked in order to change the subject.

"I run my own industrial dry cleaning business."

Crowder's face twisted. "Industrial?"

"Yeah, we cater to restaurants, butcher shops, rental stores—pretty much any business that requires cleaning services."

"Do you mind if I have a look around?" Jo asked.

"Sure."

Jo went out into the hallway and examined the photos on the wall. They were all of Natasha and Jeremy. She had light brown hair and a full smile. It was a pity her life had ended so abruptly.

Jo headed for the bedroom. There was a romance novel on the nightstand beside the bed. A small TV was perched on top of a dresser. The closet was overflowing with clothes. Jo did not have the desire or energy to go through them.

She went to the other room. This looked like it had been used as an office. There was a computer by the window. Dozens of white Bankers Boxes surrounded the computer table and lined the walls. Jo examined a stack of paper on top of one of the boxes. They were invoices for the cleaning business.

Jo looked at the shelves and spotted some nursing books. She was about to move away when something on the very top shelf caught her eye. She picked the item up. It was an ID badge.

Jo's eyes widened.

She realized she had just found the missing link.

THIRTY-EIGHT

The moment Rhodes entered Wilmington, a feeling of nausea swept over him.

His mind was bombarded with memories.

Rhodes gripped the steering wheel and kept his eyes focused on the road ahead. He drove past a boarded-up building that used to have a convenience store on the ground floor. Rhodes had spent a significant part of his childhood there, hustling cheap cigarettes and booze to any passerby.

He drove past an alley where he and a group of his friends would play marbles. It was supposed to be an innocent game, but Rhodes made his friends bet on the outcome of the game. The only way you could play was if you had cash.

He drove past a park where Rhodes had kissed Meghan O'Hara, his first girlfriend. The park was also where police had arrested him for drinking in public.

Rhodes was a troublemaker even before he was a teenager. However, when he hit puberty and had a growth spurt, he had begun to bully those around him.

Rhodes's knuckles turned white as he tightened his grip on the steering wheel.

He blamed his father for his behavior. The man had never worked an honest day in his life, and Rhodes had vowed never to see him again.

He feared what he might do to him if he did.

He was grateful that the girl was with him. She might be able to defuse his rage.

He drove until he stopped in front of a trailer home. There were other homes similar to it, but something told him it was the one he was looking for.

There were two large American flags on the roof. There was a peace symbol hanging from the window, with a Confederate flag hung next to it.

A Harley Davison motorcycle was parked out front.

Rhodes got out of the Malibu. The Harley was in pristine condition. The side decal had a rifle with the letters *SR* emblazed on it. Rhodes knew what the letters stood for: *Sullivan Rhodes*. Shooting out of the rifle were the words RHODES TO FREEDOM.

He had seen that decal on various vehicles when he was young. It was his father's moniker.

Suddenly, the trailer door swung open.

A man stepped out. He had on a cut-off T-shirt, faded jeans, and black cowboy boots. His head was covered with a yellow bandana, and he had a bushy white beard.

He was holding a rifle.

"If you're looking to buy, then that baby is not for sale," the man said, aiming the rifle at Rhodes. "If you are looking to steal it, then you came to the wrong place, boy."

Rhodes did not flinch. "Sully, put the gun away," he said.

The man stared at Rhodes for what felt like a minute but was probably less. A smile crossed his face. "You lost a lot of weight," he said. He lowered the gun. "I knew you'd come, Marty."

Rhodes wished he had a weapon on him. He would have shot Sully between the eyes and said it was in self-defense.

Rhodes had had numerous opportunities to hurt the man who had robbed him of his childhood, but he never did. Just as a parent could not hurt their child, no matter how bad they were, a child could not hurt their parent, no matter how much they had wronged them.

Tess came out of the car.

"Who's she?" Sully asked.

"She's nobody." Rhodes turned to her. "I told you to stay in the car."

"I have to use the bathroom," she said.

"I'll drive you to a gas station after I'm done."

"I have to go *now*," she pleaded.

"She can use mine," Sully said.

Rhodes hesitated. "Fine, but be quick."

Tess disappeared inside the trailer.

Sully did not come near Rhodes. They did not have a normal father-and-son relationship, which meant hugging or even shaking hands was out of the question.

"How're you doing, son?" Sully asked, eyeing him up and down.

"Fine," Rhodes replied. He did not bother asking his dad how he was doing. He did not care. "Your buddy, Barry, dropped by when I was having a drink. I'm sure you told him where to find me. How did you know I would be in Bridgeton?"

"Angie told me."

When Rhodes was in Parish, his ex-wife had asked about his father. She was probably still in contact with him.

"Barry wants his three grand and he thinks I have it."

"Well… why don't you come inside and we'll talk about it over a couple of beers."

"I'm not staying."

"Come on, son. It's been what? Twenty years since I last saw you? I mean, I did see you in the newspapers after what happened in Newport, but not in the flesh, you know."

"I'm not interested."

"Come on. We'll talk about the good old days."

"There weren't any."

Tess came back out. "Get in the car," Rhodes ordered her.

"Thanks for letting me use the washroom," Tess said.

Sully smiled. "You're welcome."

"Tell Barry to leave me alone," Rhodes said.

He went back to the Malibu.

"I need your help, Marty. I don't have his money."

"Sell that motorbike and pay him back. It's simple."

Sully's voice rose. "If it was that simple, I would've already done it." He then lowered his voice. "I didn't want to go to Barry, but I owed money to people worse than him. Plus, I don't have many prized possessions, except for that bike. And I wanted to give it to you when you got out of prison. As a gift, you know."

"That was years ago, Sully. I don't ride anymore. And quite frankly, I don't want anything from you."

"I can't just sell it, Marty. It's already got the family name on it."

"It's got *your* name on it," Rhodes shot back. "Get rid of it."

"Marty, listen to me." Sully inched forward but stopped when he saw Rhodes's hands turn into fists. "Listen, son. Can you help your old man out, just this once?"

Rhodes got in the car and drove away.

THIRTY-NINE

They were gathered in a conference room on the main floor of the FBI office. Walters, Jo, Crowder, Tarik, Irina, and Chris were seated around a large table.

Walters put her hands together and said, "What do we know so far?"

Jo said, "When I was looking through the second victim's house, I found this." She placed an ID badge on the table. "Natasha Wedham was a former employee of BMCI."

"You mean, the Bridgeton Mental Care Institute?" Walters asked.

Jo nodded. "What's interesting is that Silvio Tarconi, the first victim, also worked at BMCI. His ID badge was found in his apartment."

"Did they know each other?" Walters asked.

"I showed Wedham's photo to Tarconi's neighbors," Irina replied. "None of them had ever seen her at the building, or with Tarconi."

Crowder said, "Even Wedham's boyfriend, Jeremy Turnbull, had never seen Tarconi before. And he also said that Wedham didn't like talking about her time at BMCI. In fact, whenever he brought up the topic, she fell silent."

Walters said, "Just because they didn't meet outside, doesn't mean they never worked together."

Chris said, "I looked into their employment history. Tarconi started working at BMCI before Wedham. But for two years, they were both employed at the same time. However, Wedham left BMCI before Tarconi did."

"What did they do at BMCI?" Walters asked.

"Wedham was a nurse, and Tarconi was an orderly," Chris replied.

"That explains it!" Jo exclaimed.

"Explains what?" Walters asked.

Jo stood up and walked over to a white marker board. She wrote down the name of the victims and the messages on their bodies. Jo pointed to Tarconi's name and said, "The first victim was an orderly who had the power to control patients who got out of hand. Hence the message on his chest: *WHAT THE HANDS TOUCH*."

Jo pointed to Wedham's name. "The second victim was a nurse and thus administered medication or kept an eye on the patients' health. Hence the message on her back: *WHAT THE EYES SEE*. I believe the killer is a former patient of BMCI. As the orderly, Tarconi must have been harsh or cruel to him. Therefore, the killer cut his hands off. The nurse, Wedham, must have ignored his pleas for help or had looked the other way when he was abused. Instead of caring for his wellbeing, she was complicit in his harsh treatment. Therefore, the killer removed her eyes to punish her. Whoever is doing this wants to hurt those who had hurt him."

"So we find this former patient and we find the killer," Tarik said.

"Exactly," Jo said.

Walters turned to the group. "We already have had two dead bodies on the train. Make sure there isn't a third one."

Outside the conference room, Jo found Crowder on his phone. He looked distressed.

"Everything okay?" she asked.

"Um… there is something I need to sort out," he said. "Why don't you go to BMCI and I'll meet you there?"

"I already called. The chief administrator has left for the day. We're supposed to see him first thing in the morning."

"Okay, great. I'll see you then."

He walked away.

FORTY

The ride back from Willington left a sour taste in Rhodes's mouth. He wished he did not have to see Sully's face. The old man had aged. Twenty years would do that to anyone. Rhodes had aged as well, but Sully looked frailer than the last time he had seen him.

Rhodes gritted his teeth. *Why am I thinking about him? The man is a parasite.*

Rhodes let out a long sigh. He knew the answer to his question. Sully was his father. He was the only link he had to his past. A person could choose their friends, but they could not choose their parents.

"Was that your dad?" Tess asked.

Rhodes did not reply.

"He seemed nice."

"You don't know him, and I don't want to talk about him."

Rhodes wished it was that easy. He had tried to forget the man who had made him do things on the wrong side of the law. Maybe that was why Rhodes had chosen to become a policeman. He wanted to right the wrong of his childhood.

Sullivan 'Sully' Rhodes was a career criminal. He had robbed banks, sold counterfeit goods, laundered money, and even run a Ponzi scheme. He tried to go legit but lasted only a month or two before a new scheme popped into his head. The man thought he would one day be a millionaire from his wild ideas, and he fed the same nonsense to his son.

Rhodes could not entirely blame him, though. Sully's father was no better. During Prohibition, he smuggled booze from Canada. He was always in and out of prison. He was caught for racketeering, illegal gambling, and even human smuggling. Rhodes never learned how his grandfather had ended up doing the latter. Eventually, his grandfather's vices got the better of him. In Las Vegas, he stole money from the wrong people. His body was found behind a dumpster. He had been shot eleven times. The rumor was that it was mob-related. Rhodes never knew the man. He had only met him once, and that was when he came to see Sully for money.

Rhodes had tried to go down the right path, but it did not work out. If he thought about it, *his* crime was worse than any his father and grandfather had committed. He was a convicted murderer.

Maybe crime ran deep in the blood of the Rhodes men.

Rhodes was driving up to the house when he spotted a man and a woman standing by his apartment door.

"Oh-oh, that's my mom and her boyfriend," Tess said.

They parked and got out.

"Tess, go inside the house!" Tess's mom yelled.

Tess lowered her head and walked away.

"You're gonna get it tonight, little girly," the boyfriend hissed.

The mother turned to Rhodes. "What're your plans with my daughter? She's a minor, you know."

"I didn't know she was in the car."

"You wanna tell that to the cops?"

"Yeah, do you?" the boyfriend added with a smirk.

"I don't," Rhodes replied.

"Good. Then stay away from Tess," the mother said.

"I will, just as long as your boyfriend stays away from her."

"What did you say?" The boyfriend got in Rhodes's face. He was several inches shorter than Rhodes, and Rhodes had more than several pounds on him.

Rhodes said, "If you touch her, I will hurt you."

The boyfriend laughed. "You mind your own business."

The mother said, "Tommy has never tried to touch my girl."

"That's not what Tess said."

"You shut your mouth," the boyfriend snapped. "Or else I'm gonna have to teach you a lesson."

"Have you ever killed anyone?" Rhodes asked.

The boyfriend blinked. "What?"

"Have you ever put a gun to a man's chest and pulled the trigger? Have you ever killed a man in front of his entire family?"

The boyfriend stammered. "I... I..."

Rhodes closed in until he was inches from the boyfriend's face. "Well, I did, and I spent ten years in prison for it, so you don't scare me." Rhodes turned to the mother. She had suddenly turned pale. "If I find out that anything happened to Tess, I will burn the house down with you both alive in it. Do you understand me?" Rhodes's voice was even and composed, giving it an almost sinister tone.

The mother and her boyfriend rushed inside.

FORTY-ONE

Jacopo walked down the street. Night had fallen and he enjoyed being out by himself. It was not like anyone knew who he was. If they did, they would be terrified of him.

The media had begun to dub the deaths the "Train Killings." Jacopo was not partial to the name. He just found it funny how the media wanted to sensationalize the murders.

There was speculation that there were going to be more dead bodies. *There will be*, he thought, *but it all depends on my master*.

His master had given him life, and he would tell him whose he should take.

He watched as people passed by him. He relished the fact that he could snatch any one of them from their safety and security. This knowledge gave him strength and power. But he had his orders. They did not involve harming anyone who was not a target.

His master decided his victims. And tonight, he knew, there would be another name.

He looked forward to it. It gave him a sense of purpose.

He wished he could see who his master was. He would mark his body with his master's image. It would be his way of thanking him for what he had done for him. But his master preferred to stay in the shadows. His master had chosen him for a reason: to be his sword of justice.

These people had wronged his master, and it was Jacopo who would teach them a lesson.

But this was just the beginning. His master had a grand plan, and Jacopo was at its forefront.

He passed an electronics store. Several televisions were on display in the front windows. One of them was playing the news. The reporter was talking about the Train Killings. There was no volume, but he could read the subtitles.

Ellen Sheehan spoke of a serial killer who was preying on the citizens of Bridgeton.

He was offended. He did not consider himself a serial killer. He was not deranged or psychotic. He did not have a traumatic childhood. In fact, his childhood was filled with joy and happiness. His parents were educated, and they were married until they died of old age. He was loved by his parents, and he loved them in return.

He was not a product of his upbringing. He was a product of his life's decisions.

As an adult, he had made choices that took his life down a path of destruction. Serving his master was his way of returning to a life of fulfillment.

Ellen Sheehan signed off. Jacopo did not like her. She was cocky and arrogant. She felt like she could dictate *his* story. She did not realize she was just a pawn in his master's plan. Without him, she would still be covering dog shows.

He hoped one day his master would make her his next target. He would take great pleasure in slicing her up.

But he did not know who the next victim would be until he received his instructions.

He looked at his watch. It would be soon. Very soon.

FORTY-TWO

Jo stared at the clock on the wall. With each turn of the hand, her face became darker and darker.

She was in the office of Dr. Stanley Freeman, Chief Administrator of the Bridgeton Mental Care Institute. Freeman was tall, striking, and black. He wore a gray suit with a white tie.

He tapped his finger on the oak desk before him.

Jo was waiting for Crowder. She had already left him several messages. Seeing the impatient look on the chief administrator's face, she said, "My partner is running late, I think it might be better if we got started."

Freeman leaned forward and placed his elbows on the desk. "I can honestly say I am shocked by what you've just told me. I had no idea the victims of those terrible train murders once worked for BMCI."

"You didn't know them?" Jo asked.

Freeman shook his head. "They must have been employed before my time."

"How long have you worked here?"

"As of next month, it'll be ten years."

Jo frowned. *The victims were employed before his time*, she thought.

"Can you pull up all files on Silvio Tarconi and Natasha Wedham?"

"Yes, of course."

"Can you also give us files on your current and former patients?"

Freeman paused. "The files on Mr. Tarconi and Ms. Wedham you can have. They are dead, after all. But I'm afraid I can't release files on our patients. Those are confidential. You'll need to get a court order."

Jo leaned forward. "Dr. Freeman, we have two former employees of this institution who were brutally murdered. Someone out there is exacting revenge, and we now have a strong suspicion that it could be a former patient. We believe there may be more victims. Before another one of your employees meets the same fate, I would advise you to cooperate with us."

"What you want me to do is hand over people's psychological history," he said. "A lot of people, some even prominent, have passed through the gates of this building. The only reason they've done so is because they know their secrets will be safe with us. I cannot break their trust."

Jo said, "I understand the position you're in, but we have a duty to protect the public. The sooner we capture this killer, the sooner the public will be safe."

Freeman stood up and walked to the window. "There has to be some other way for you to conduct your investigation."

"There isn't. The only way we can identify a suspect is to know their motive. We do know the train victims were not chosen at random. They were targeted, and their bodies were marked with messages. From these messages, we strongly believe something must have happened at the institute that provoked their killer into taking deadly actions."

Freeman let out a long sigh. "You will have to give us some time. We've had hundreds, if not thousands, of patients come to our institute. Digging up old files will not be easy."

There was a knock at the door, and it opened. Crowder popped his head through the crack. "Sorry I'm late," he said, out of breath.

Jo said, "Detective Jay Crowder is working on the case with me."

Freeman nodded.

Crowder came over and sat down next to her. "What did I miss?" he whispered to her.

Jo ignored him and said, "Please continue, Dr. Freeman."

"Like I was saying, the files are stored in our basement. It could take days for us to go through them."

"We don't have time. We need those files as soon as possible. In fact, Detective Crowder will be more than willing to assist you in your search."

Crowder looked at her. "I will?"

"Yes, you will," Jo replied. "Dr. Freeman and I waited almost half an hour for you before we started our meeting. It is only appropriate you make up for the lost time."

Jo could tell Crowder was not happy about doing grunt work, but she did not care. She was not his partner, nor did she have to cover for his poor punctuality.

She felt like they were running against the clock. They needed all hands on deck.

Her only wish was that they were able to find a name in those files before the killer struck again.

FORTY-THREE

Rhodes found Tess standing next to his Malibu. "How long have you been standing there?" he asked, curious.

She shrugged. "Not long."

He waited for her to leave so that he could get in his car.

"Thanks," she said.

"For what?" he asked.

"For whatever you did. My mom and her boyfriend were scared when they came back into the house. They haven't said anything to me so far. In fact, they've kind of been okay with me. My mom even made me breakfast."

Rhodes nodded.

"Where are you going?" Tess asked.

"Work."

"Can I come with you?"

"No."

"Then, I'll sit outside your front steps."

Rhodes looked up at the sky. The clouds were gray, and it looked like it was going to rain.

He wanted to ask Tess why the skies were always gray. "Why don't you just stay at home?" he said instead.

"Even though it's okay right now, I'm still not comfortable being around my mom's creepy boyfriend."

Something occurred to Rhodes. "Don't you have school?"

"It's summer, duh?" she said, rolling her eyes.

Right. "What about your friends? Can't you hang around with them?"

"One has a job and the other is visiting her grandparents in another state."

Rhodes realized Tess had no place else to go. "Why don't you go to the library?"

"It's so boring," she complained.

"I have a lot to do," Rhodes said, unlocking the front door. "I have to go."

"Fine. I'll just sit outside in the rain. I'll probably get wet and maybe get sick. But that's okay. You go do your work."

Rhodes blinked. Was she using reverse psychology on him? Or was she trying to make him feel guilty?

There were several reasons why he did not want any children. One reason was that you could not win an argument with them.

"Fine. Get in."

Tess clapped her hands and squealed like a little girl.

On their way to Rhode's destination, they grabbed something to eat. Rhodes was hungry, so it was only polite to offer some to Tess.

Rhodes parked the Malibu and looked across the road.

"Why are we stopping here?" Tess asked, sipping her drink through a straw.

Rhodes nodded towards a pizza shop. "We're keeping an eye on that place."

Tess made a face. "If you wanted pizza, why did you get burgers and fries?"

Rhodes was not good at making up stuff. Plus, she was old enough to know how the world actually worked, so he decided to tell her the truth. "You see that kid over there by the corner?"

"Yeah, the one who's dealing drugs."

Rhodes looked at her. "How did you…?"

"I may be a kid, but I'm not stupid. I see things all the time. You should drop by my school. I can show you the exact places you can get high."

"Well, I need that kid over there to sell me some drugs."

Tess gave him a look. "I didn't think you were into that, but you do live alone, so yeah, it's possible."

"I'm not a user."

"Sure. That's what they all say."

"I'm really not."

Tess smiled and winked. "Okay, gotcha."

Rhodes shook his head. If he wanted to keep his sanity, he had to learn to stop arguing with a teenager.

"Why do you want to buy drugs anyway?" Tess asked.

"I need it as leverage against the owner of the pizza shop."

"So go buy it."

"The kid won't sell it to me."

"Why not? You got money, right?"

"He thinks I'm a police officer."

Tess gave him a once over. "If I didn't know you, I'd think you were a police officer too. But when I spoke to Olya, she mentioned you were in prison before."

"The landlady told you?" he asked.

"I talk to her sometimes when I'm outside waiting for my mom."

"And you're not worried about hanging around with a convict?" he asked.

"I did an internet search on you. I didn't want another creep hanging around my house. You wouldn't believe how much stuff is written about you."

"So you know who I am?"

"Former Newport Police Detective Martin Rhodes."

"So, you know what I did?"

"Yep. And I would have done the same thing too. I'm glad that creep got punished for what he did to that little boy."

Rhodes looked out the window and then faced her. "Tess, what I did was wrong. I paid ten years of my life for it. No one has the right to take another person's life, not even me. Do you understand?" His tone was dead serious.

She stared at him and then nodded. "Yeah, I hear you."

He turned back to the pizza shop.

"Anyways," she said, as if what happened a few seconds ago was water under the bridge, "I know your background, so that's why I didn't mind hiding in your car, you know. I know I would be safer with you than at home with my mom's boyfriend."

"Be careful who you trust," Rhodes said.

"Plus, I got something if you or anyone else got any funny ideas."

She put her hand in her small bag and pulled out a can of pepper spray.

"Where'd you get that?" he asked.

"I ordered it online."

"You know how to use it?"

"Yep. I've tested it a couple of times."

"Good," he said, turning back to the shop.

"So, what's your plan?" she asked.

"I don't have one—yet."

"Okay, fine. I'll go buy it," she said.

"What?"

"Yeah, if he won't sell it to you, then he'll definitely sell it to me."

Rhodes shook his head. "I'm not going to send a minor to buy drugs."

"I'm not really going to buy it. I'm not stupid, you know."

"It could be dangerous."

"You'll be watching me the entire time."

Rhodes frowned.

"Let me help you. It's the least I can do for what you did for me."

Rhodes thought about it. "I still don't think it's…"

"Just trust me, okay? I've got a plan."

Rhodes sighed. He really had no other options. Plus, by now, he should know better than to argue with her.

FORTY-FOUR

The conference room at the FBI field office was filled with boxes containing files from the Bridgeton Mental Care Institute.

It was tedious and time-consuming work, but with Tarik, Irina, Jo, and Chris going through each patient's file, the task had been cut in half.

Crowder had been excused. He had lugged all the boxes from the institute to the FBI building, after all.

He sat on a chair and just watched them. He was still sweating and out of breath. There was a moment when he thought he would have a heart attack. His face was beet red, and he felt a sharp pain in his chest. To his relief, it turned out to be acid reflux.

The team culled through the contents and created a profile of the killer.

Jo said, "White male, between the age of twenty-five and forty-five, was at the institute ten to fifteen years ago, around the time of Silvio Tarconi and Natasha Wedham's employment, and he is in relatively good shape."

"Why in good shape?" Crowder asked between breaths.

"He carried the first victim from the platform and into the train. The only way this was possible is if the killer was in good condition."

"Unlike Mr. Universe over here," Chris said, nodding toward Crowder.

"You try carrying fifteen boxes, why don't you?" Crowder shot back.

Irina pulled out a file. "Ken Lieberman, age thirty-one, was at the institute thirteen years ago, when he was eighteen."

Chris pounded a couple of laptop keys and said, "He lives in Bridgeton, but I don't think he's our guy."

"Why not?" Jo asked.

"Lieberman's driver's license shows that he is close to three hundred pounds."

"What's the date on the license?"

"It was renewed last year."

Jo shook her head.

Tarik pulled up a file. "James Salley. Age thirty-eight. He was at BMCI almost twelve years ago."

"Why was he there?" Jo asked.

"Post-traumatic stress disorder."

"From what?"

"Time served in Iraq."

"I'm on it," Chris said, typing away at his keyboard. "Salley also lives in Bridgeton. He works for the Port Authority, but his medical records show he is still on heavy-duty anti-depressants. And he weighs one-eighty and is close to six feet tall."

"He fits the description," Jo said. "Anyone else?"

Irina said, "Mathias Lotta. He was at BMCI almost fifteen years ago, when he was only fourteen years old. He left when he was eighteen."

"Where is he now?" Jo asked.

"Dead," Chris said. "He was in a car accident a few years after he left the institute. The car was found in flames, and his body was inside."

"Okay, next."

Tarik said, "Joshua Havelen. He was at BMCI almost thirteen years ago, when he was only sixteen. He was released when he was twenty-one."

"Where is he now?" Jo asked.

Chris frowned. "There is no record for him for almost ten years. No employment history, no driver's license—nothing."

Jo said, "Tarik and Irina, find out what you can on Joshua Havelen. In the meantime, Crowder and I will go speak to James Salley. With his military background, he might be who we are looking for."

FORTY-FIVE

Tess got out of the Malibu and crossed the road. She approached a kid leaning on a brick wall next to the pizza shop. The kid wore a sweatshirt emblazoned with the name of a local basketball team, a baseball cap, and baggy jeans that hung low on his waist.

The kid had his eye on Tess the moment he spotted her. It was his job to evaluate who was a client and who was a cop.

"Hey, how's it going?" Tess asked as she got near.

He nodded. "What's up?"

"I heard I can get some pot here?"

"Where did you hear that?"

"At school."

"Where do you go?"

She gave him a name.

He paused and then said, "My cousin goes there. He didn't send you, did he?"

Tess did not know his cousin, or if he had a cousin who went to her school. He was obviously testing her. If she lied, he would see right through it and send her off.

She shrugged. "I don't know who you're talking about. But can you help me or not? I can go elsewhere, you know."

He smiled. "Whoa girl, chill. I was just conversing. You got money?"

Rhodes had given her a few bills for the transaction. "Sure."

"Show me."

She held out her hand.

"Okay, put it away," he said, looking around. "How much you want?"

"Whatever I can get with what's in my hand."

The kid laughed. "What're you, a junkie?"

Tess frowned. "I just need some right now, okay?"

He did not stop laughing. "Sure, girl, no problem. Stick your hand out like you are shaking my hand." She did, and he quickly extracted the money from her palm. "I'll be back with your goods."

The kid walked to the front of the pizza shop and went inside.

A few minutes later, he returned. His right hand was closed into a fist, but Tess could tell he was holding something inside.

The kid looked around. "Now, I'm going to shake your hand and then you're going to walk away. Got it?"

Tess nodded.

The moment the exchange was complete, a car pulled up.

A man got out.

"Oh, my God!" Tess said. "It's my dad."

The kid froze.

"What do you have in your hand, missy?" Rhodes said.

"Nothing." Tess tried to hide it.

"Show me," Rhodes said in a stern voice.

Tess held out her hand. It contained a small bag filled with pot.

Rhodes glared at the kid. "Are you selling weed to my daughter?"

"I never gave her that," the kid said.

"I saw you give it to her," Rhodes replied.

The kid turned to walk away. Rhodes grabbed him by the collar.

"Let go of me," the kid said.

"I want to talk to your boss," Rhodes demanded.

"I didn't do nothing."

The kid tried to squirm away, but Rhodes held on tight.

"If I don't talk to your boss, I'll call the cops. You'll go to jail for selling drugs to a minor. Do you want that?"

The look on Rhodes's face told the boy he was not lying. "No, I don't," the kid said.

"Then let's go," Rhodes said. He turned to Tess. "Get inside the car. I'll deal with you later."

FORTY-SIX

The house was at the end of the street. It was a double-story with a single garage. The lawn was mowed, and there was a neat flower bed.

A minivan was parked in the driveway.

Someone's home, Jo thought as she got out of the car.

Crowder was with her. "When was the last time you pulled out your weapon?" Jo asked him.

He shrugged. "I can't remember."

Jo was not pleased with his response. Crowder probably had not fired his weapon in years. She would have to be even more vigilant as they approached the house.

They went up the steps and rang the bell. Jo kept her hand on her weapon. Crowder did the same, but she could tell he was just doing it because of her.

The door opened and a woman poked her head out. "Can I help you?"

"Is this James Salley's house?" Jo asked.

"Yes, it is," the woman replied.

"Is Mr. Salley home?"

"He's on the back porch."

Jo flashed her credentials. Crowder fumbled for his badge.

"Is Jim in trouble?" the woman asked. "I'm his wife."

"No, we would just like to ask him a few questions."

"Give me a minute." She disappeared into the house and then returned and said, "You can go around to the back. The side door is open."

Jo and Crowder went through a narrow path and found James Salley seated on a lawn chair with a beer bottle in his hand. He had a buzz-cut hairstyle and was clean-shaven. He wore a large sweatshirt, white khaki pants, and black military boots.

"James Salley?" Jo asked.

"That's me," he replied. He did not get up to greet them. "My wife just told me you guys wanted to ask me some questions. What is this about?"

Jo pulled out two photos and showed them to him. "Do you know them?"

Salley squinted at them. "No. Should I?"

"They worked at the Bridgeton Mental Care Institute when you were a patient there."

A smile crossed Salley's face. "Is this about the bodies on the train?"

Jo glanced at Crowder. They locked eyes for a brief moment. She then turned back to Salley. "So, you're familiar with the case?"

"Only what I see on the news."

"Did you know them?" Jo asked.

He sighed. "I may have seen them when I was at the institute, but I can't be sure. I was on some serious medication."

"Why were you at BMCI?"

"After my tour ended in Iraq, I had a mental breakdown. I was diagnosed with severe PTSD. I thought the government would take care of me, but they did shit-all. They referred me to some group that helped veterans up in Montana. I spoke to them a few times on the phone, but I was too messed up to make the trip. My wife—she was my girlfriend at the time—paid for my visit to BMCI. She saved my life. Once I started feeling better, I proposed to her right away. We now have two beautiful kids."

Jo said, "Can someone confirm your whereabouts for the past couple of days?"

He frowned. "I guess so. I went to work and I came home. You talk to my supervisor, and my wife will vouch for me."

"Do you use the subway?"

"I drive," Salley replied. "I drop the kids off at school and take the minivan to work. My wife takes the bus. But no, I don't take the train."

"Can you give us your supervisor's number?" Jo asked.

"I have his card in the house. Let me go get it."

He stood up quickly.

Jo and Crowder reached for their guns. Salley raised his hands. "Whoa, take it easy. I'm not armed." He slowly put the beer bottle down.

Jo relaxed. "Sorry, a force of habit."

He walked to the door with a slight limp.

"What's wrong with your leg?" Crowder asked.

He pulled up his pant leg, revealing a prosthetic. "Why do you think I was taking medication? After I lost my leg, I thought I was incomplete. It took a lot of therapy and my wife's love to make me realize that losing a limb didn't define who I was."

The killer does not walk with a limp, Jo thought.

Salley was not the one they were looking for.

"We're sorry to take your time, Mr. Salley," Jo said.

FORTY-SEVEN

Rhodes was in a small office in the back of the pizza shop. Next to him was the owner: a short, balding, heavyset man.

When Rhodes had come in with the kid, the owner denied having anything to do with him. Hearing this, the kid started to cry. He must have realized he was on his own and that he would be going to jail.

The kid begged to be let go. He wanted to go home to his mother. Rhodes felt sorry for him. He was still a teenager, after all.

The owner, on the other hand, did not budge. He kept saying he had nothing to with the kid.

Rhodes found himself in a difficult position. He offered the owner an alternative. "Okay, if you give me access to your shop's security footage, I will forget what just happened. The kid can go on dealing, and I won't show my face at this establishment again."

The owner had quickly nodded.

"How far back do you want to go?" one of the owner's employees asked.

Rhodes gave him the date Reed's phone had sent its last signal.

"I don't know if we can go back that far."

"Go check," the owner said.

The employee left.

The owner smiled at Rhodes, exposing a gold tooth. "I'm sure we have what you're looking for."

"I hope so," Rhodes replied.

"We will, we will. I never throw videos out," the owner assured him. "The people I deal with can't be trusted." Rhodes knew he was referring to other drug dealers and drug addicts. "If any of them got any bright ideas, or try to steal from me, then I have them on tape. You know what I'm saying, right?"

Rhodes nodded.

"And if I give you the video you want, you will forget about our misunderstanding, right?"

"Yes," Rhodes replied.

The owner turned to the kid. "No hard feelings, okay? This is business, you know."

The kid did not say anything. Rhodes could tell he was thinking about how quickly the owner was willing to throw him under the bus. Rhodes hoped the kid had learned a lesson and would change his career path.

The employee returned. He was sweating and out of breath. He held a VHS tape in one hand. "I found it," he said.

The owner turned and gave Rhodes a smile. "I told you we had it."

The employee popped the tape in a player and let it run. The security system was vintage 1990s. All VHS, no DVD. The employee had to fast-forward the tape through hours of footage until he reached the section Rhodes was interested in viewing.

Rhodes glanced at his watch.

The owner said, "You're not a police officer, right?"

Rhodes shook his head.

"You should think about becoming one. You have the look of a police officer."

"I'll think about it," Rhodes replied dryly.

The employee stopped the tape and played it at normal speed.

Rhodes saw the front of the shop. There were several people lounging by the windows, but one stood out. He was wearing a long T-shirt and baggy jeans. His hair was pulled back into a ponytail, and he wore a heavy gold chain around his neck. A cell phone was in his hand, and he looked agitated as he paced back and forth.

The last signal from Reed's phone had come from the pizza shop. The punk had to be the one Rhodes was looking for.

He disappeared from view, returning a short time later. He then went inside for a few minutes and reemerged, holding a slice of pizza and a can of pop. He took a bite and left.

"Rewind it," Rhodes said.

The punk reversed back into the shop, came out empty-handed, disappeared, and then reappeared a few seconds later by the front windows.

"Play it," Rhodes ordered.

Rhodes watched the footage again at normal speed.

"Stop it right there," he said.

Rhodes shoved his hand in his coat pocket. The owner and his employee jumped in their seats. They let out a sigh of relief when Rhodes pulled out a piece of paper. He checked something on it and then focused on the TV monitor.

There was a running clock at the bottom of the screen. The time the punk had gone to order pizza was around the same time Reed's phone had lost its signal, give or take one minute.

The punk had just disposed of the phone. Rhodes was now most likely staring at the man who had killed Reed Yates.

FORTY-EIGHT

Rhodes walked out of the pizza shop with not only a photo of the suspect but also his name. Alfonso Guzman was a small-time drug dealer who sometimes bought his supplies from the pizza owner.

Guzman owned a barbershop at the other end of the city, which was way out of the pizza shop's distribution zone, but the pizza owner did not mind wholesaling drugs to a competitor. All he cared about was the almighty dollar.

Now Rhodes was stuck in a dilemma. If he gave the name and photo to Tim Yates or Detective Crowder, they would want to know how he got it. This meant he would have to tell them about the pizza shop. Rhodes had given his word to the owner that he would not mention the shop in exchange for the information he just received.

Rhodes detested having to make deals with drug dealers. *But I did it to capture a murderer*, he told himself. The police had had no breaks and Rhodes was no longer working within the confines of the law. He did not have to follow policies or procedures. He was a consultant, as Tim Yates had called him. He was hired to do a job, and that was to find who was responsible for Reed's murder.

It was not Rhodes's job to arrest the killer, nor did he have any authority to do so. It was his job to point the police or his employer, Yates, in the right direction, and right now, it was pointing to Alfonso Guzman.

There was another problem that prevented Rhodes from going to either Yates or the police. He did not have any substantial evidence linking Guzman to Reed's murder. He had him at the location but nothing more. Even if Crowder brought Guzman in for questioning, he could deny any involvement in the crime.

What if it was not Reed's phone in Guzman's hand? What if the real killer had disposed of the phone and Guzman found it? What if Guzman had bought the phone on the black market, not knowing who it had belonged to? There were too many what-ifs.

When Rhodes returned to the Malibu, Tess said, "Did you find what you were looking for?"

"I did and I didn't," he replied, sticking the key in the ignition.

"I don't understand."

"I have the information, but I don't know if I can use it."

"Okay, so are we, like, back to square one?"

"Not exactly."

He put the car in gear.

"Where are we going?"

"I want to check out something."

FORTY-NINE

When Jo and Crowder returned to the office, they found Tarik and Irina waiting for them.

"How'd it go?" Tarik asked.

"Nothing," Jo replied. "James Salley was a dead-end. Did you find anything on Joshua Havelen?"

"We did, but you're not going to like it," Tarik replied. "After Havelen left BMCI, there is no record of him, at least not in the U.S. We were able to find a nine-year-old police report from the Mexican authorities that a car belonging to Havelen was found in the Mexican state of Chihuahua, across the border from Texas."

Irina said, "I then spoke to US Customs and Border Protection, and they confirmed there is a record of Havelen crossing through the border at Fort Hancock, Texas and into El Porvenir, Chihuahua, but they have no record anywhere of Havelen returning to the U.S."

Jo frowned. "So, he might still be in Mexico."

"Looks like it," Tarik said.

"This means he might not be our suspect," Jo said.

"That's why I said you won't like what we found."

Jo sat down at her desk and rubbed her temples.

"We did, however, speak to Ken Lieberman," Tarik said.

Jo looked up. "Who?"

"The patient who was close to three-hundred pounds."

"And?"

"Lieberman is divorced and single. In fact, I think he was lonely. He was more than willing to speak to us. We asked him about Silvio Tarconi and Natasha Wedham. Lieberman said he remembered them. They were never mean or abusive to him, but they were mean to Mathias Lotta."

"He was the one in the car accident, right?" Jo asked.

"Yep. According to Lieberman, Lotta was a nice kid. He wasn't sure why he ended up at the institute in the first place. He was so young. He kept to himself and he only ever spoke to Havelen. I guess they both were teenagers, so they hit it off."

"I'm not sure how this helps us." Jo felt a headache coming on. "One is dead and the other has disappeared to Mexico."

FIFTY

The camera was pointed at Ellen as the male talk show host asked his next question. "Ellen, why do you think the Train Killer chose to contact you?"

Ever since Ellen had discovered the second victim, she had sort of become a celebrity in Bridgeton. Her producer, Miles, was not happy she had kept her conversation with the killer from him. But he knew reprimanding her would not be a smart move. For one thing, more people were now tuning into her segments. Naturally, Dan Ferguson was quickly pushed aside, but it was not Miles's decision. It was his boss's. She now wanted to make Ellen the face of the evening news.

Ellen paused, giving her best smile for the camera, and said, "I don't know why, really. I hope it's because I am truthful in my reporting."

The talk show was on the same network, so her superiors thought it would be a boost to ratings if they had her do the rounds on all their affiliate programs. Ellen knew they were using her. But what they did not realize was that she was using them too. She was getting her name out.

Before the Train Killings, only a small portion of Bridgeton knew who she was or what she did. Now they knew her by only one name: *Ellen*. She hoped to one day have her own show, where she and other reporters investigated hard-hitting topics. She wanted to be taken seriously, and nothing was more serious than covering a serial killer.

The host said, "When do you think the killer will contact you next?"

She wished she had an answer. So far, the killer had used her as a puppet to get his sick and twisted message across. She did not mind being a mouthpiece, but she wanted to have some control over the message.

She paused again, as if she was contemplating the question, and said, "I hope the killer never contacts me." This was a lie. She was praying for the call every day. "This means that there won't be any more victims," she continued.

The truth was that viewers wanted more dead bodies. The more sensational the crime, the more people craved it. This was not her fault. Society was depraved. She just reported what was happening around her.

"I also hope that the police are able to capture this evil person," she said.

The killer had been a Godsend. Without him, she would still be fighting for stories.

Plus, she was now more popular than Janie Fernandez. This was more satisfying than anything else.

The show ended. Ellen quickly moved away from the stage. She had no interest in chit-chatting with the host.

Her cell phone buzzed.

The number was blocked.

She answered the call. "Ellen Sheehan."

"I enjoyed your interview," the voice on the other end said.

Ellen's back arched. It was the same deep voice of the killer. *He must have been watching the show*, she thought.

"Why are you calling me?" she said, but then realized it might have come across as too harsh.

"I'm calling to tell you there will be another dead body."

"I'm not interested in playing your games," she said.

There was silence. Then the voice said, "I hope you realize there are others who would *kill* to be in your position right now. In fact, you should be grateful to me for what I've done for your career."

"You want me to thank you, is that it?" she asked. "You called me because you knew I would go above and beyond to get your message across, and I've done it. Now I need you to do something for me."

There was silence. Ellen hoped she did not overplay her hand. She could not afford to lose this.

"Okay, what do you want?"

"I want to meet you."

"You know that's not possible."

"There won't be any police. You have my word."

"As much as I would like to, I just don't trust you."

"Then, you tell me when and where."

He was silent a moment.

"I'll call you to set up a time and place."

The line went dead.

FIFTY-ONE

The neighborhood was the opposite of affluent. There were boarded-up shops with signs still hanging above the windows. There was a pawn shop, a cash-back outlet, and even an employment center. The latter seemed just for show. If the center was able to assist the locals with jobs, the impoverished area would look far different.

Rhodes pulled into a plaza, and after driving around the parking lot, he spotted the barbershop. There were several people inside, and one was standing by the door, smoking a cigarette.

Rhodes did not dare go near it. He did not want to blow his cover yet.

He drove around and parked in front of a used clothing store.

"What're we doing here?" Tess asked.

"We're interested in that." Rhodes nodded in the direction of the barbershop.

"You need a haircut?"

Rhodes was about to say something when an idea formed.

"Actually, I do need a haircut," he said, looking in the review mirror. Ever since he got out of prison, he had only gotten his hair trimmed once. There were now long strands of hair that he had to constantly pull behind his ears.

"Okay, that's weird," Tess said. "If you'd told me that. I would have shown you some barbershops that were closer to our house."

Rhodes looked around and then pulled out a five-dollar bill. "There's a convenience store over there. While I get my haircut, why don't you grab something for yourself?"

"Are you trying to get rid of me?" she asked.

"I'm trying to keep you busy while I get my haircut. I mean unless you want to stay in the car."

She snatched the bill from his fingers and said, "I'll see you back in the car."

He watched her get out and head to the convenience store.

He could not believe he was playing babysitter.

He got out and headed for the barbershop.

When he entered, he found all eyes on him. There were maybe four people in the shop. One was on the cutting chair with another doing the cutting. Two were lounging in the chairs in the waiting area.

None of them was Alfonso Guzman.

A man came up to him. He was black. "Can I help you?" he said.

"I need a haircut."

"Sure," the guy said. "Have a seat."

Rhodes sat down.

"How do you want it?" the guy asked.

"Trim the sides, please."

The guy got down to it and asked, "I haven't seen you around this area."

"I just moved here."

"Where're you staying?"

On his drive over, Rhodes had spotted a cluster of buildings. "I got an apartment two blocks from here."

"Right," he said, understanding.

A few minutes later, a car pulled up to the shop. It was a white Escalade. Through the mirror, Rhodes caught Guzman coming out. He was accompanied by a bigger man.

He entered, gave his buddies in the shop fist bumps and high fives, nodded at the guy cutting Rhodes's hair, and, without even glancing at Rhodes, he and the bigger guy disappeared in the back.

"All done," the guy said.

Rhodes looked at himself and nodded.

He paid the guy and left.

At the Malibu, he found Tess waiting for him. She was drinking a smoothie with a straw. "You find what you were looking for in the barbershop?"

"Who said I was looking for anything. I wanted a haircut."

"Sure, whatever." She got in the car.

Tess may still be a teenager, but she is a good observer, Rhodes thought.

And she was right. He did find—not what—but *who* he was looking for.

Alfonso Guzman.

FIFTY-TWO

Every lead they looked into had so far been a dead end. Jo knew there would be another dead body, and it was only a matter of when.

They were running out of options, so she had decided to go see the family of Joshua Havelen, the patient who had disappeared in Mexico.

She found his mother and sister in a town about an hour's drive from Bridgeton.

Jo was now seated in their living room with a cup of tea before her.

"When was the last time you spoke or met Joshua?" Jo asked.

The sister, whom Jo had found out was three years older than Joshua, said, "Joshua had dropped by to visit my mom right after he got out of the institute. We had wanted to go pick him up, but he insisted he would come see us instead. I think that was almost ten years ago, but the last time we heard from him was a few years after that."

The mother spoke. "I think something horrible has happened to my son."

"Why would you say that?" Jo asked.

"Josh would never miss my birthday. Never. Even when he was at the institute, he asked them to let him come and visit me on my birthday. I think he is dead."

Jo did not know what to say.

The sister said, "After he got out, we tried contacting him, but we couldn't. We even went to the police to report him missing, but they said they couldn't help us because he was old enough to go wherever he wanted. Plus, there were rumors that he had gone to Mexico."

Jo opened her mouth to ask them about that.

The mother said, "He didn't go to Mexico."

"Why do you think that?" Jo asked. "His car was found across the border."

"He didn't know anyone there. We were a close-knit family. When he disappeared, it affected my husband terribly. He had a fatal heart attack. He died a broken man."

"I know this a personal question, but why was Joshua admitted to the Bridgeton Mental Care Institute?"

The sister said, "My dad was a big baseball fan, and so he wanted Josh to take up the sport. Josh joined the pee wee league, and he worked his way up the ranks, but we could tell he wasn't interested in any sports. He only did it for my father. He played hard and practiced hard, but when he couldn't even get into the minor leagues, he felt like he had disappointed my dad. That's when things started to fall apart. He started doing drugs, drinking heavily, and he started hallucinating."

"He was only sixteen when he was admitted, right?" Jo said.

"Yes, my parents knew something was wrong, but they thought it was only a phase he was going through. They thought he was acting out like most teenagers did at that age. They thought he would grow out of it. But it only got worse. One day we got a call from the police that Josh had apparently stripped down to his underwear and had run across the field at a Major League baseball game. We didn't believe it until we saw it on the news. We had no choice but to put him in the institute, or else he would've been charged with mischief or maybe something worse. We didn't realize that, at the institute, his mental health was only going to deteriorate. If we had known, we would have found some alternative form of health care service."

"Why do you think his health deteriorated?" Jo asked.

"It was that other boy," the mother said. "He ruined Josh."

"Who?"

"He was at the institute with Josh."

Jo thought a moment. "Do you mean Mathias Lotta?"

"That's him." The mother's eyes filled with rage. "It felt like he was controlling my son."

"How so?"

"When Josh came by to visit us after he got out, the other boy was with him. We thought that was odd, but Josh insisted the boy was his friend. The boy never left us alone, not even once. He watched Josh as if Josh was under his spell. There were times I asked Josh a question, and the boy would answer for him. I should have thrown that boy out of the house, but I was glad to see my son. I wanted him to get better. I wanted my family to be complete again."

The mother choked up. Her daughter put her arms around her.

Jo said, "Unfortunately, Mathias Lotta is dead, so we can't question him."

Silence fell over the room.

Jo realized it was time to go, but she had one more question to ask, and she did not want to sugarcoat it. "Do you have any reason to believe your son may have come back to Bridgeton to take revenge for what happened to him at the Mental Care Institute?"

The mother shook her head. "If Josh was in Bridgeton, he would have come to visit me. I know my son. But he hasn't. And that tells me that he is dead."

FIFTY-THREE

Ellen left the studio and took the elevator down to the basement. The parking garage was full at this time of day. Normally, she would be able to find a spot near the doors, but this morning she was late, and she had to park her Prius at the other end of the row.

Her eyes were glued to her cell phone. She was catching up on stories from her competitors.

So far, no one had had a breakthrough in the Train Killings case. *Why should they?* She thought. *I'm the only one who has had direct contact with the killer.*

She had still not heard from him. He was supposed to let her know the time and day of their meeting.

Patience was not one of Ellen's strong suits. She wanted everything right away. Money. Fame. Power. She wished she had it all right then.

What if the killer decided not to follow through? What if he decided to bail on me? After all, he owed her nothing. His actions had already gotten him enough attention. She needed him more than he needed her.

She had a feeling he knew this too well. Maybe it was why he was letting her sweat it out.

Regardless, whenever he would call, she would be ready for him.

She pulled out her keys and unlocked the doors.

She got in and put her purse on the passenger seat.

When she pushed the key into the ignition, she felt something cold touch the back of her neck.

"Don't turn," a voice said from behind.

Startled, Ellen swallowed hard. She glanced at the rearview mirror, but it was smashed. Even the side-view mirrors were not useful anymore.

"Put your hands on the steering wheel," the voice said.

Ellen did as instructed. "You didn't have to do that," she said, trying to regain her composure. "It'll cost me good money to fix."

"You wanted to meet, so you have to pay the price." The voice did not sound mechanical, like on the phone, but it was still heavy and low.

She could feel the barrel of the gun dig deep into her skin.

"I'm here now," the killer said. "Ask me your questions."

"Why are you killing those people?"

"I have my reasons."

"You have to give me more than that."

"I'm doing it to send a message."

"To who?"

"To someone."

"And what message is that?"

"That I'm going to right the wrong."

Ellen wanted to face him, but the gun prevented her from doing so. "Who wronged you?" she asked.

There was silence.

"Many people," he replied.

"Your victims, did they wrong you?"

"Yes."

"Were there others?"

"Yes."

"So, there will be another body on the train?"

"Yes."

"When?"

There was silence.

Ellen's mouth was dry but she wanted an answer. "When will there be another body?"

"Tomorrow."

She heard the sound of the gun being cocked.

Her heart began to beat faster. Sweat rolled down her back. Her knees began to vibrate uncontrollably. "What are you going to do to me?" Her voice quivered.

"I want you to close your eyes and slowly count to ten. If you decide to look back, you will be dead before you do so. Do you understand?"

She nodded. "Yes."

She closed her eyes and began counting when she heard the back door open and close.

She was not about to deviate from his instructions. She did not dare look behind her.

FIFTY-FOUR

The house was stylish and modern. It was made of glass and steel. It was unlike any building Rhodes had ever seen, but the design made sense because the house belonged to architect Tim Yates.

Rhodes walked up the narrow path, all the while admiring the structure.

He rang the doorbell and waited. A few seconds later, through the glass panel next to the door, Rhodes saw a woman appear.

She opened the door and said, "Can I help you?"

She was tall, blonde, and attractive. She had no wrinkles on her face, but her neck was a different story. The woman was much older than she made herself up to be.

She was likely Tim Yates's wife—Reed's mother.

"My name is Martin Rhodes," he said. "Mr. Yates asked me to drop by."

"Oh, yes, Tim told me," she said. "You're helping us find who…" She paused to compose herself. "…took Reed away from us."

He nodded.

"Tim is in the back. He's been waiting for you."

She took him through the house, which was even more eye-catching than the outside, and into the backyard.

Yates was sitting on a patio chair next to the pool. He wore a light sweater, white khaki pants, and loafers.

He held a drink in his hand.

He stood up and shook Rhodes's hand. "Would you care for a drink?"

"No thanks, I'm fine," Rhodes replied, taking a seat opposite him.

Yates got straight to the point. "As you can imagine, I've been waiting anxiously for some news."

Rhodes did not have a cell phone. If he did, he could have avoided the trip over here by making one call instead.

When Rhodes had taken the case, he had assured Yates that he would give him regular updates. He had paid Rhodes five thousand in advance, after all.

Yates continued. "I didn't know how to contact you, so I was seriously thinking of returning to the bar where we last met."

There was a reason Rhodes was hesitant in getting a cell phone. Now he knew why. He did not want people calling him every minute of the day for updates. People did not realize that crime was not solved in one hour like on most television shows. It was a lot of grunt work and most of it never panned out. It could be days, months, even years before there was a break in an investigation. In fact, back in the Newport PD, there was an entire room filled with boxes of unsolved cases, and some belonged to Rhodes. Such was the nature of the business.

Rhodes said, "I will not run away with your money, Mr. Yates."

"I'm not concerned about the money," Yates said. "I'm concerned about finding who killed my son."

"I've made progress in the investigation," Rhodes said.

"Do you have a suspect?" Yates asked.

Rhodes hesitated, but then said, "Yes."

Yates sat up straight. "Have you gone to the police?"

"Not yet. I need more evidence before I hand over all the information to the authorities."

"Just give me a name," Yates said eagerly.

"And what will you do with this name?"

"I… I don't know, but I would like to know who took my boy's life."

"I'm sorry. I can't."

Yate's eyes widened with surprise before they flashed with anger. "Am I not paying you for a name?"

"You are."

"Then why won't you tell me?" Yates was fuming. "Is this about money? Do you want more?"

"No. I'm sufficiently compensated."

"Then what is it? Why won't you tell me the bastard's name that killed my only son?" Yates was now on his feet.

"Do you own a gun?" Rhodes said calmly.

Yates blinked. "Yes. But why is that important?"

"If your son's killer was standing before you right now, would you shoot him?"

Yates paused. He blinked some more and then sat down. "The right answer would be no, but who knows how any parent would react at such a moment."

"I have already paid a steep price for my actions, and I wouldn't want you to make the same mistake. I need to confirm a few things, and when I do, you will have your son's killer."

Yates thought about it and then nodded. "When will you have a name for me?"

"Soon," Rhodes replied. "Very soon."

FIFTY-FIVE

The moment it was safe, Ellen called the FBI. They had instructed her to drive straight to their office. Ellen was now seated in Charlotte Walters's office. It was medium-sized with windows on one side and a wall with certificates and medals on the other. In the middle was a desk. Behind it was the FBI seal with the words *Department of Justice, Federal Bureau of Investigation* encircling it. In the middle of the seal was the FBI motto: *Fidelity, Bravery, Integrity*.

Ellen was familiar with it, having read about it when she was young. The choice of colors, the selection of images, and the overall design of the seal represented what the bureau stood for. No matter how many times she had seen the seal, she always found it imposing and awe-inspiring.

Walters sat across from her but did not say anything.

Ellen tried to keep her attention on the objects in the office when the door swung open and Johanna Pullinger entered. Ellen had met her before, and she found her to be no-nonsense and straight-to-the-point.

"We reviewed the footage from the parking lot. Unfortunately, we didn't find anything that might help us," Pullinger said.

"Are you saying no camera caught him?" Ellen said.

"Your car was parked on the other end of the lot," Pullinger replied. "The way the camera was pointed resulted in a small blind spot. The killer must have known this, or why else would he choose to meet you today and not any other day?"

"What about when he left?" Ellen asked.

"There is footage of a man walking out of the parking garage. But he was wearing a hoodie and baseball cap. Never once did he look up. He does fit the description of the killer. This tells us you were telling the truth."

Ellen's face twisted in shock. "Why would I lie?"

Walters said, "The question we have is, why would you tell us the truth?"

"Why wouldn't I?"

"You have hid information from the authorities before. Who's to say you are not working with the killer."

Ellen's mouth dropped. "He put a gun to my neck. I thought I was going to be one of his victims."

Walters did not say anything.

Ellen continued. "Plus, if I wanted to, I would have kept this information to myself."

Walters stared at her and said, "And he told you there will be another body on the train tomorrow?"

Ellen nodded. "Yes."

"Did he tell you when?"

Ellen shook her head. "No. Before I could ask another question, he left. He threatened to shoot me if I looked back. I was not going to do anything stupid."

Pullinger turned to Walters. "Both bodies were found in the morning. We can assume the next one would be at that time as well."

Ellen said, "So do we have an agreement?"

When Ellen had contacted the FBI, she told them she had information on the Train Killings and she would share it with them on the condition that the bureau gave her exclusive access to the scene.

Walters said, "If you turn out to be correct, only then do we have an agreement."

Ellen smiled.

FIFTY-SIX

After his meeting with Tim Yates, Rhodes needed a drink.

After he ordered a whiskey, a voice from behind him said, "I'll pay for that."

Rhodes turned and found Barry Kowalski. He had a smile on his face, and Rhodes knew this was not going to be good.

"I'll have a glass of what he's having," Barry said. He sat next to Rhodes on the right.

Barry's bodyguard, whose name Rhodes still did not know, took the stool to Rhodes's left. Like before, they had boxed Rhodes in.

His drink came and Rhodes calmly took a sip of it.

"I have to give it to you," Barry said with a smile, his gold tooth visible. "I never thought you hated your old man so much that you would not help him out."

Rhodes said nothing.

"You and he used to be a team before."

"That was a long time ago," Rhodes replied.

Barry nodded. "I get it. It was before you went legit."

Barry's goon had ordered a bottle of beer. To impress Rhodes, he removed the cap with his teeth. He smiled at him. His left canine tooth was missing.

"What do you want, Barry?" Rhodes asked, annoyed. He was hoping to have a drink in private.

"I don't want anything," Barry replied. "I'm just here celebrating. Do you want to know why?"

Rhodes did not.

"Should we tell him?" Barry asked his bodyguard.

The bodyguard smiled. "Yeah, we should."

Barry leaned closer to Rhodes. "We just beat the shit out of your old man."

Rhodes's face turned hard.

Barry laughed. "Actually, my man did most of the damage. I just slapped him around for fun."

Rhodes's jaw tightened. "You didn't get your money?"

"We took the motorcycle, of course. Your old man wasn't too happy about it, but what choice did he have? But there was the matter of my reputation, you know. If your old man had paid on time, I would have left him alone. When I had to go to his shithole of a home myself and get what belonged to me, well, I had to teach him a lesson, you know."

Rhodes took a deep breath. It was not his problem. Sully should not have gotten involved with them in the first place. *He deserved what he got*, Rhodes told himself.

He calmly took a sip from his glass.

Barry said, "I wish you were there, boy. You could've heard your old man squeal and beg for mercy."

Rhodes saw red.

He took a deep breath and calmly finished his drink. He held the glass in his hand. He turned to Barry. "You must feel real proud beating up an old man."

Barry's smile disappeared. "I thought you hated your old man."

"I do," Rhodes said. "But I hate bullies even more."

Before Barry could react, Rhodes smashed the glass across his forehead. Barry fell back, holding his face. In the next instant, Rhodes kicked back hard with his heel. The stool the bodyguard was sitting on slipped from underneath him. The bodyguard hit his head on the side of the bar.

The bodyguard tried to stand, but Rhodes kicked his face with the back of his boot. Blood spurted out of his mouth as he collapsed to the ground.

Rhodes put his boot on Barry's chest and held him down. He was ready to take a swipe at him when a voice warned, "Stop this now!" It was the bartender, and he was aiming a rifle at Rhodes. "Get out before I put a bullet in your head."

Rhodes's lips curled into a frown. He was beginning to enjoy coming to this bar. Now he would have to find another one.

He wiped his hands on his coat and left.

FIFTY-SEVEN

Jo was back in the office of Dr. Stanley Freeman. She had rushed to BMCI the moment Ellen Sheehan had left the FBI office. What Sheehan had told them put the FBI and the local police on high alert. There would be another victim on the train tomorrow.

Jo could feel the pressure in her chest, but she could not worry about the added stress on her heart. She and her team were working against the clock. They had to stop another person from losing their life.

Even though they still did not know who the killer was, they did know how he chose his victims. They had all worked at BMCI.

It was why Jo was back at the institute. She wanted all current and former employees to take extra precautions. They should not come to work alone or be home alone. But more importantly, they should avoid staying out at night. The killer could strike at any time.

Freeman was on the phone. He looked anxious. "Are you sure?" He listened. "Please double-check."

"What's wrong?" Jo asked.

Freeman cupped the receiver. "Our Human Resources Department has contacted all our employees on file, except for one."

"Who?"

"Doug Curran. He is our resident psychiatrist. He's not picking up his phone, nor had he come to work today."

Jo moved closer. "How long has he been employed at BMCI?"

Freeman asked the HR person on the other end. He listened and then said, "Curran has been at BMCI for almost twenty-two years."

Jo's eyes narrowed. "This means he was here when Silvio Tarconi and Natasha Wedham were employees of the institute." Jo stood up. "Can you give me his address?"

Freeman asked the HR person and then jotted it down on a notepad.

With a piece of paper in hand, Jo left BMCI in a hurry.

She drove like a madwoman. She had a bad feeling in the pit of her stomach. On her way out, Freeman had said that in twenty-two years, Curran had always informed the institute whenever he would be absent.

Jo did not believe in coincidences. The killer had warned there would be another victim. All his victims came from BMCI. Curran was at BMCI at the same time the first two victims were, and now he was nowhere to be found.

The house was located in a gated community. She drove up to the front entrance, and a guard came over.

She flashed him her credentials, and he immediately opened the gates for her.

She drove into a newly paved road and passed neatly manicured lawns. The houses were big and opulent. They were probably close to a million dollars.

Curran not only worked at BMCI but also in his private clinic. *The money must be good for him to afford a place here*, Jo thought.

She pulled up to a gray brick bungalow. There were already two cars parked in the driveway. One was a white BMW and the other a black Mercedes-Benz.

Jo squinted.

The killer also drove a black Mercedes.

She pulled out her weapon and approached the front door. She peeked through the living room window. The lights were still on inside.

The occupants are home.

She thought about ringing the bell but quickly decided against it. She did not want to alert the killer if he was still inside.

When she touched the door handle, the front door swung inward.

It's not locked?

This was not good.

She moved into the hallway. Her steps were long and deliberate. She kept her eyes on her surroundings. She listened for sounds and looked for shadows.

If she heard anything or spotted anything, she would take swift action.

She moved through the living room and into the kitchen.

When she got close to the marble island, she spotted something. It was a pair of feet, and they were lying on the tiled floor.

She slowly and carefully peeked over the edge of the island. A female body was on the floor, facing down. There was blood on the tiles.

Jo leaned over and placed two fingers on the woman's neck. There was no pulse. The woman was dead.

She moved around the house, checking the rooms, hallway, and even the garage.

When she was satisfied it was empty, she put her gun away.

She then called forensics and sat down on the sofa.

A moment later, the front door swung open. Jo reached for her gun but then stopped. It was the same guard who was at the gate.

"Is everything okay?" he asked.

Jo shook her head. "There's a body in the kitchen."

The guard went over and then came back. "That's Mrs. Curran," he said.

"Where is Mr. Curran?" Jo asked.

"I don't know," the guard replied.

"His car is still parked out in the front," Jo said.

"He must still be here."

"He isn't. I checked the entire house." She then thought of something. "You guys screen everyone who comes in, right?"

He shook his head. "Not everyone, only the guests and visitors. The owners have their own access cards."

"Then how can someone go missing?" she asked.

The guard thought about it and then said, "My shift started an hour ago. Let me call the guard that was here before me."

He dialed a number, spoke a few words, and then hung up. "The guard said he had seen Mr. Curran leave the gates to go out for a run."

"When was this?" Jo asked.

"He said it was in the morning."

Jo frowned.

"Maybe Mr. Curran will come back later," the guard added.

Jo knew better. She was too late.

FIFTY-EIGHT

Jacopo watched as Doug Curran wept like a little girl. He had snatched him while the man had gone for his morning jog. It was not that difficult.

Jacopo had driven up to him to ask for directions. Curran did not suspect anything, and why would he? Jacopo was in a Mercedes-Benz. All the neighbors drove high-end vehicles.

The moment Curran came near the Benz, Jacopo was able to sedate him. A dart gun filled with a tranquilizer was concealed underneath a piece of cloth.

Jacopo sharpened the blade and then paused. He waited until the noise of the train had gone away before he continued sharpening.

Curran squirmed on the table. His mouth was duct-taped, and his hands and feet were restrained.

Jacopo did not know why his master had chosen Curran, and quite frankly, he did not care. His master had given him specific instructions, and he did not want to deviate from them one bit.

He held the knife to the fluorescent tube. It glistened in the light.

He was ready.

He stood up and walked over to Curran.

There was a puddle of tears underneath Curran's head. He was crying uncontrollably.

Jacopo leaned closer to Curran's ear and said, "I'm going to remove the tape from your mouth. If you scream, it will do you no good. No one will hear you. This room was chosen because it is buried deep in a labyrinth of tunnels. Do you understand me?"

Curran nodded.

"Okay, good."

Jacopo stripped the tape off.

Curran screamed at the top of his lungs. Jacopo was not fazed. He half expected it.

He waited until Curran's face was red and he was out of breath.

"Are you done?" Jacopo asked calmly.

Curran's chest moved up and down as he sucked in air.

"You can keep screaming, but you'll only be delaying the inevitable."

Curran swallowed and said, "Why are you doing this?"

Jacopo shrugged.

"Please, let me go."

"I can't," Jacopo replied. "I have my orders."

"Don't hurt me. I haven't done anything to you."

"You're right. You haven't done anything to me. In fact, until today, we hadn't even met before."

"Who are you?"

"Is it important?" Jacopo asked.

"My name is Doug Curran. My wife's name is Claudia Curran. She's waiting for me at home."

Jacopo knew Curran was a psychiatrist. He also knew Curran was trying to make this personal in the hope that he would feel sorry for him and let him go.

Jacopo smiled. "Your wife is not waiting for you. She's dead. I killed her."

Curran's face contorted in anguish. He began to cry again.

After snatching Curran, Jacopo had used the fob on his key to get through the front gates. The guard was too busy reading the newspaper to notice him. Even if he did, the Mercedes's windows were tinted, so he had no idea what he looked like. Plus, Jacopo had fake license plates on the vehicle. He would toss them out once he completed his task.

Mrs. Curran was collateral damage. He feared she would call the police when her husband did not return. His master wanted Curran's body on tomorrow's train. Jacopo needed enough time to set everything up according to his master's instructions.

"Now open your mouth and stick your tongue out," Jacopo said, raising the knife.

Curran shut his mouth tight.

"We can do this the easy way or the hard way. Your choice."

Curran shook his head.

Jacopo sighed. *Why didn't they learn fighting him will only make things worse?* he thought.

He picked up a thin metal piece that had a sharp pointy end. He stuck it in Curran's body, just below the ribs.

Curran clenched his jaw. Tears flowed down his cheeks as he tried to endure the pain.

It is a waste of time, Jacopo thought. He twisted the metal piece.

Searing pain shot through Curran's entire body. He tossed and thrashed, but he refused to open his mouth.

Jacopo pushed the metal piece further and twisted it even more.

Curran's face was beet red. He opened his mouth and let out a long scream.

Jacopo carefully grabbed his tongue with a pair of pliers.

He pulled it as far as it would go.

He smiled.

He held the knife up in the air. "I'm afraid, doctor, after tonight, you won't be very useful in your profession."

Curran's eyes widened. They were filled with sheer terror.

FIFTY-NINE

The FBI and the Bridgeton PD had stationed agents and officers at the entrances and exits of all subway stations.

They could not shut down the transit system. That would result in chaos and gridlock on the city streets. Bridgeton Transit Authority kept the city moving. Plus, the mayor did not want a serial killer holding the citizens hostage. He did not want his city to be gripped by fear.

They should find the killer, and they should punish him for his evil crime, he reminded the authorities. Or else heads would roll.

Jo felt the pressures in her chest again. The one place she could not afford to have it.

If Dr. Cohen found out, he would make her take a leave of absence. *Not now*, she told herself. *Not when the city is being terrorized by a killer.*

Jo was at Dupont Station, Tarik was at Wellington Station, Irina was at Chester Station, Crowder was at Broadview Station, and Walters and Ellen Sheehan were at Sherbourne Station. The killer had used each of these stations for his purposes. There was a remote chance he would risk using them again, but their theory was that he might want to use familiar locations for his drop-off and then eventually escape. Plus, with over forty subway stations, there was no way they could be everywhere. The BTA employees were also put on high alert, so there was some help. The more eyes there were, the better they had a chance of spotting the killer.

Jo watched as each passenger moved through the turnstiles. Anyone walking hand-in-hand, or anyone pushing someone in a wheelchair, or anyone looking like they were homeless was her target. She was also interested in anyone with a hoodie or baseball cap.

She tried to spot anything out of the ordinary, but as time went by, more and more people entered and exited the station.

With rush hour upon them, her task had suddenly become even more difficult.

SIXTY

Paul Roopsingh sat in the conductor's cab as the train moved along. His family had come from Guyana when Paul was only two years old. He had grown up in the United States and considered himself as much an American as he did Guyanese.

When he saw an opening at BTA, he jumped at the opportunity. After working for BTA for fifteen years, Paul enjoyed every minute of his job.

That day, however, he felt differently.

When his supervisor had called and told him about the police presence at each station, he had seriously considered calling in sick. He knew something bad was going to happen. *Why else would the police be there?* he thought.

He had a sinking feeling there would be another body on the train. He shivered at the thought. Why anyone would do something like that was beyond him.

Paul was married with two pre-teen children. He could not imagine them growing up without a father. He did not want to be involved in whatever was going on at work that day. In fact, when he told his wife, she was adamant he not go to work. But he could not just take time off so suddenly. If he did, someone else would have to cover his shift. And it would be one of his friends.

Over the years, he had worked with a lot of BTA employees who were now his friends. He knew their spouses, their girlfriends, their boyfriends. He had even gone out drinking with some of them. When his children were born, one of his friends had covered for him, and another friend had taken over his train the day he had to leave work due to his mother's untimely death after suffering a fall at home.

Family.

That was what the employees of BTA were to him. There was no way he would abandon his shift today.

As the conductor, Paul's duty was to make sure that all the passengers had gotten on and off the train before he closed the doors. It was not a very difficult job, but it did require him to be alert and attentive.

There were always people rushing to catch the train before the doors closed. At times, they would shove their foot, arm, or backpack between the doors in order for them to stay open.

Naturally, this would delay the train from moving ahead, but he had come to realize this as part of his job. He stopped being angry at the hurried passengers. No one liked waiting, especially when they could get to their destination earlier.

The train pulled into the station. Paul immediately stuck his head out from his cabin. He turned a switch, and the train's doors opened.

Paul watched as passengers exited the train. This allowed him to keep an eye out for anything or anyone suspicious. But with rush hour, it made his task challenging.

When the passengers had entered the train, he closed the doors.

He waited, but the train did not move. Normally, when everything was clear, the train engineer would take the train to the next station.

Then the telephone rang in his cab. He picked up the black receiver and listened. It was the train engineer. Apparently, there was a problem with a train on another track, and they needed to reroute their train.

Paul hated when this happened, but such occurrences were part of his job. They were operating an old and antiquated train system, and problems like these were a daily occurrence.

He pressed a button and spoke into the receiver.

He announced to the passengers that the train would be out of service at the next station. This meant they would have to vacate the train at that time. He knew there would be much grumbling, some cursing, and he would have a few expletives hurled in his direction, but there was nothing he could do about it.

Orders were orders.

When the passengers had gotten off at the next stop, he locked his cab and began his walk through each compartment to make sure the train was indeed empty.

In the second to last compartment, he noticed a man sitting on one of the seats. He was wearing a large coat, and his chin was resting on his chest.

Another sleeper, he thought. There were many in the morning. Some were so deep in slumber that even announcements over the public address system did not wake them. Others would cover their ears with headphones or earpieces to block out all sound.

He moved closer to the man. "Sir, the train is out of service."

The man did not stir.

"Sir, you have to get off," he said.

The man kept his head low.

Damn, Paul thought. *I will have to wake this guy up.*

The moment he touched the man's shoulder, he fell forward onto the floor.

Paul knelt to help the passenger up.

He quickly straightened up, his eyes wide with horror.

The man was lying on his side with his mouth wide open. Paul could clearly see that the man was missing something.

He stepped away from the body and reached for his walkie-talkie.

SIXTY-ONE

Jo could not believe she was back at the station's security office, seated next to Dennis Wilmont.

The call had come from a BTA employee. The body was discovered on a train that had just dropped off passengers at Greenwood Station. Walters was on her way there now. Jo should have rushed there too, but she had more important things on her mind.

How did the killer drop off the body and then disappear? The FBI and BPD had secured all the entrances to the subway.

The killer was bold and dangerous. Even though he knew the law was looking for him, he still risked capture and did what he had said he would do.

What kind of game is he playing? Jo thought. *Is he trying to taunt the FBI or the BPD? Is he trying to make us look bad? What would he gain by doing that?*

Jo dismissed such thoughts. Law enforcement was not the killer's target. He was committing murder to make a statement directed at the people at BMCI.

They had hurt him, and now he was hurting them.

The institute had been put on lockdown. Their employees and their patients had been told to stay within the institute's walls. An extreme measure, but this was an extreme circumstance. The safety of the BMCI employees was their number one priority.

The BTA officer scanned through the footage. Jo was not watching any of it. She was still thinking of the killer.

So far, all the suspects were overweight, handicapped, missing, or dead. None of them fit the profile. Maybe it was their profile that was incorrect. Maybe they were not looking at the case from the right angle.

The BTA officer said, "I think I found it."

Jo blinked. Her attention focused on the monitor.

"That's Woodbine Station," he said.

On the screen, a man wearing a baseball cap and colored overalls was pushing a garbage container on wheels.

"Is that a BTA uniform?" Jo asked.

The supervisor shook his head. "I can't be sure from the footage, but I doubt if we mistook him for an employee."

The man wheeled the container to the middle of the platform. It was empty. The time on the screen indicated it was well before rush hour.

The man looked around and then removed two garbage bags from the container. He looked around once more to see if the coast was clear. He then reached inside the container and pulled out a body. He propped it up beside a pillar. He looked at his watch and waited until the train pulled into the station.

One of the BTA employees, most likely the conductor, stuck his head out of a window. Jo could tell the employee could not see the man or the body as they were shielded behind the pillar. The employee checked one end of the platform, and when he turned to check the other, the killer lifted the body up in his arms and ran inside the train. It happened in a matter of seconds. Then the doors closed and the train left the station.

Jo did not need to see what happened next. The killer placed the dead body on a seat and most likely got off at the next stop.

"Do you want to see more?" the supervisor asked.

Jo shook her head. "Just send a copy to the Bridgeton FBI field office."

She felt a powerful headache coming on.

SIXTY-TWO

Rhodes was parked outside the barbershop. He could see Guzman was inside. He never once picked up a scissor and cut hair. He left that task to the man who had given Rhodes a haircut.

Guzman is far more interested in dealing drugs, Rhodes thought. Perhaps the barbershop was a front to peddle the drugs, just like the pizza shop was. Regardless, Guzman was now laughing with some of his regular customers. None of them were there to get their hair cut.

Rhodes rubbed his chin. Tim Yates was already anxious to find his son's killer. His patience would run out if Rhodes did not come up with a name soon. But Rhodes wasn't even sure if Guzman was the man he was looking for. All he had was his gut instinct and footage from the pizza shop.

He needed to act quickly. But what could he do? He could not waltz into the shop and accuse Guzman of murdering Reed. He would get beat up for something like that, or worse, get shot.

It was at moments like these that made Rhodes wish he was still a lawman. The badge gave him some immunity when it came to dealing with people like Guzman. They would think twice before assaulting an officer.

Things were different now. He could not arrest Guzman and take him down to the station for questioning. Guzman's buddies would be on him before he even touched Guzman. Rhodes could handle himself, but he would not be able to explain his actions to the police. They would want to know why he had attacked Guzman in the first place.

Rhodes had to find another way. He had to do it without being physically involved.

He had an idea. He was not sure if the idea was good or if it would even work, but it was worth a shot, given the circumstances.

He looked around and spotted a phone booth in the corner of the plaza: a one-minute walk from the barbershop. Plus, it had a clear view of the shop and its inhabitants.

Rhodes walked up to the booth, grabbed the receiver and stuck some coins in. He read the telephone number posted outside the barbershop and dialed.

A few rings later, he saw the guy who had cut his hair answer. "What's up?" he said.

"I need to speak to Alfonso," Rhodes said. He referred to Guzman by his first name to keep the conversation informal.

"Who is this?" the guy replied.

"My name is not important, but I need to speak to Alfonso."

"Well, he's not here."

Rhodes could clearly see he was lying. Guzman was lounging on one of the barber chairs. "Okay, fine," he said. "I'll just go tell the police what I know. When Alfonso finds out, he'll be pissed at you."

"No! Wait!" the guy replied.

Rhodes saw him turn to Guzman. After they exchanged a few words, Guzman grabbed the receiver.

"What's up?" Guzman asked.

"I know what you did," Rhodes said.

Guzman made a face. "Who's this?"

"Like I told your friend, my name is not important. What is important is that I know what happened to Reed Yates."

"Reed who?"

"The kid you shot."

Rhodes saw Guzman jump out of his chair. "I don't know what the hell you're talking about, but if you have any balls, you come and say that to my face, tough guy."

"I don't need to say it to your face. All I need is to tell it to the police."

Guzman laughed. "Go ahead. Tell them your lies. Let's see if they believe you."

"They won't believe what I say, but they'll believe the photos I took of you dumping the phone behind the pizza shop." Rhodes was bluffing, but he was willing to take a risk.

Rhodes could see Guzman was startled. He ran his hands through his hair and he began pacing the shop.

"You're lying, man," he said.

"I'm not. Reed Yates came to you to get his phone back. You and he got into an argument, and you shot him. I'm sure you didn't mean to, but he's dead. You then got rid of the evidence. I will tell the police what I know. They'll track the phone to the pizza shop. That's where the last signal came from before you destroyed the phone. They'll also have my photos to back up what I'm saying. This will give them enough ammo to make you suspect number one."

Guzman was irate. He stomped his feet, and he looked like he was ready to hurl the phone at the wall. His buddies were not sure what was going on.

Guzman finally calmed himself. "Okay, okay. You want something, right? Isn't that why you called me?"

"I want ten grand."

"No way," he spat. "I don't carry that kind of money."

"Then we've got a problem," Rhodes replied.

"You gotta come up with a reasonable number, man," Guzman complained.

"You're a drug dealer. You handle cash all the time. Plus, what is ten grand when you could be facing life in prison?"

Guzman rubbed his chin. "Okay, but you gotta give me some time to get the money."

"I need the money right away."

"When?" he asked.

"Tonight," Rhodes replied.

"That's too soon, man. It's just not possible."

"It's tonight, or I go straight to the police tomorrow morning."

Guzman sighed. "I'll see what I can do."

"Just have the money."

"Okay, where?"

Rhodes gave him an address.

He hung up and watched as Guzman rallied his buddies. Even from where he was standing, Rhodes could see they were carrying weapons.

There was no way Rhodes would show up at that address without a plan.

SIXTY-THREE

Ellen could not believe her luck. Another body had been found on the subway. She had told the FBI about the impending murder, and she turned out to be right.

They now owed her exclusive access to the scene of the discovery.

Naturally, Walters was not happy, but she had no choice. They had an agreement.

Ellen and Walt followed Walters to Greenwood Station. There, she was escorted past the other media outlets gathered outside the station. Ellen caught Janie Fernandez standing by the entrance. She was in shock when she saw Ellen accompany the FBI inside. She was probably seething with anger right now.

Good, Ellen thought. She wanted her to stew knowing that her charm and beauty could not get her the lead story, and that it was Ellen Sheehan who had used her wit and cleverness to beat her to it.

Ellen would never confess that it was the killer who had given it to her on a silver platter. Regardless, when a gift fell in her lap, Ellen had used it to her advantage.

Walters was next to her as they moved down the stairs. They had to hurry to keep up with Walters.

"You can shoot your segment on the platform," Walters said. "But, you can't go inside the train."

"But we had a deal," Ellen reminded her.

Walters stopped and faced her. "Our deal was that we give you information on the murders before anyone else. Under no circumstance will I let you contaminate the scene of the crime."

"The scene is already contaminated," Ellen said. "There were probably dozens of passengers who were on that train with the dead body."

"As procedure, we will block off the scene," Walters said. "If you decide to cross the line, our deal ends. Understood?"

Ellen bit her bottom lip. She could keep arguing, but she already had a step-up on her competitors. Plus, she had a feeling Walters was waiting for a reason to annul their agreement.

"Understood," Ellen replied.

They reached the platform, where men and women in uniform were waiting for Walters.

"Wait here," Walters said. She walked over to a BTA security officer and exchanged some words with him. He came over after Walters boarded the train. He was big and imposing. "You can set up your camera over there," he said, pointing to the far end of the platform.

Ellen was about to oppose him when Walt put his hand on her shoulder. "I think it'll give us a full view of the platform and the train."

Ellen could tell that Walt did not want a confrontation with the officer.

She sighed. "Okay, let's go set up the shot."

SIXTY-FOUR

When Jo reached Greenwood Station, she saw Walters standing with Ellen Sheehan at the far end of the platform. Sheehan was interviewing Walters, and Jo could tell Walters was only doing it because she had to.

Jo did not envy Walters. To face the camera and explain how a killer had slipped by the FBI was not something Jo was prepared to do.

She quickly ducked under the yellow police tape and found Ben standing in the middle of the train compartment. Today he had complimented his white overalls with a bright purple watch.

Jo did not bother walking up to him. She took a seat a few rows back.

Ben walked over to her. "You don't look good, Jo," he said.

"I just need a breather," she replied.

Her skin was pale, and her forehead was beaded with sweat.

"These murders are taking a toll on you, you know," he said. "The amount of pressure you are under would've made a normal person have a breakdown, but with your heart condition, it could be worse."

"I'll be fine," she said. "You sound like my brother, you know."

"I wish I *was* your brother. I would physically remove you from here."

She looked at him, smiling. "You're really worried about me?"

He shrugged. "Sure. If anything happens to you, how am I going to find out who the real Bridgeton Ripper was."

"Tell me again why you are so interested in that case?"

"As you already know, death fascinates me. Even as a kid, I would stay up all night reading true crime stories," he replied. "Before I retire, I want to write a book that will be on par with all the great true crime writers. I want to be like Ann Rule, Vincent Bugliosi, and Truman Capote. What better chance of doing that than solving a case that is in my city, my very own backyard?"

Jo put her head back and closed her eyes. She was feeling fatigued. *Maybe I rushed over here too fast,* she thought. *A little rest would do me some good.*

She was drifting off to sleep when Ben's voice woke her up. "I would normally encourage you to take a nap," he said, "but if Walters finds you like this, she'll surely boot you off the case."

Walters was the only person in the FBI, other than Ben, who knew of Jo's condition. She had, on numerous occasions, advised Jo to step back and focus on her health.

Ben said, "As much as I want you to take a break, I don't want Walters suspending you."

"Thanks," she said.

"But Jo, take a long vacation," he said. "You've earned it after all these years. Let someone else handle the case. Or maybe even let the Bridgeton Police take this one."

Jo raised an eyebrow. "You want Crowder to lead this investigation?"

"I confess I don't like the guy. He rubs me the wrong way, but he is a detective, after all."

Jo stood up. "I'm not going anywhere until this is over."

"You have to at least slow down."

She shook her head. "There's a killer out there who is mocking us. This is the third body he's left for us to find. There is no way in hell I'm going to stop until I catch him. Now let's go see the victim."

Jo already knew the body was Doug Curran's, so she did not bother to ask Ben for the victim's ID. "What's missing on this one?" she asked him instead.

"It took me a while to find it, but I'll show you," Ben replied. With his gloved hands, he opened the victim's mouth. "The tongue has been removed."

Jo thought a moment. "He's a psychiatrist. His job is to listen to his patients and provide a professional opinion. Makes sense the killer took his tongue if he felt the psychiatrist had misdiagnosed him, or if the killer didn't agree with the psychiatrist's diagnosis of his condition." She paused a moment. "What about carvings on the body?"

"Those were a little easier to spot. I'll show you." Ben pulled up the victim's sleeve. The word WHAT was carved into the skin. The words were made using the same crude object used on the previous victims. Ben pulled the victim's collar down, exposing the upper shoulder and revealing the word THE. He then lifted the left pant leg up. The word TONGUE was carved on the leg. Finally, he pulled the shirt up and revealed the word SPEAKS on the victim's stomach.

"*What the tongue speaks*," Jo said, putting the words together.

"He's getting creative," Ben said.

And he's getting bolder, Jo thought.

SIXTY-FIVE

Jacopo was proud of himself as he drove the Mercedes at high speed down the freeway. He had completed all the tasks his master had placed before him. When he had received his last target, his master had indicated that it would be his final assignment. At first, he was disappointed. He had begun to look forward to the kills. They gave him a sense of purpose, a sense of power, a sense of control, something he had never felt before. His life had always been chaotic, unstructured, and full of despair. It had left him feeling lost and helpless. He almost wished his master would give him more to do.

But he had to remind himself of why he had done what he did. The car he was driving, the apartment he was staying in, and the money waiting in a Swiss bank account for him to collect were his rewards for a job well done.

Sure, killing those people gave him a satisfaction that no amount of money could replace, but he was not some deranged serial killer who wanted to terrorize the citizens of Bridgeton. The media had it all wrong. He was doing it to have a better future. He was doing it to get his family back.

But there was something that had nagged him throughout this process. Would his master betray him? Would he renege on their deal now that the mission was complete?

He shook his head.
No, absolutely not.

It was his master who had plucked him out of a life of obscurity and given him so much. If it was not for him, he would still be living in some dumpster, or worse, dead.

No. His master owed him nothing.

This knowledge made the task all that much easier. He trusted his master as his master trusted him. Why else would he have chosen him?

Loyalty meant a great deal to his master. He had said so on numerous occasions. Jacopo was loyal to him. And he hoped he had fulfilled his duty loyally.

It was now time to celebrate by reaping the rewards of his labor.

But before he could do that, there was one more thing he needed to do. He had to go back and clean his kill room of anything that could lead back to him. He would do that later tonight when the police were gone. It was nerve-wracking seeing them outside each station this morning. But fortunately for him, he had something that gave him access to the transit system. Once he flashed it, they let him through without a single question.

He smiled once again at his good fortune.

Life was going to be different from now on.

Craig Orton was his past, and Jacopo Manfredi, the full name his master had given him, was his future.

"*Jacopo Manfredi*" he said, letting the name roll off his tongue. He was beginning to like that name because it had a sort of ring to it.

Maybe he'd take it as his new name when he started his new life.

But he still had some unfinished business to attend to.

SIXTY-SIX

Rhodes watched as Guzman and his bodyguard left the barbershop. Rhodes was right behind them as they drove away in the Escalade.

He kept a fair distance between the two cars. Even though Guzman had no suspicions he was being followed, Rhodes still wanted to be careful.

He wanted to keep the element of surprise with him. Guzman had been rattled, and Rhodes wanted to see what he would do next.

Rhodes had a strong feeling that Guzman did not act alone and that there were others who were involved in what happened to Reed. *How did a teenager's cell phone end up in the hands of a drug dealer?* Rhodes thought. *There has to be some link*.

During his research, Rhodes found nothing that indicated Reed was involved in drugs of any kind. In fact, he was a good kid with good grades. He had ambitions of becoming an architect like his father. Rhodes did not get the impression that he would jeopardize his future by doing something illegal. But Rhodes also knew that almost everyone had secrets. Whether it was an affair they hid from their spouse, or a love child from a previous relationship they did not want the world to know about, or a fraudulent action caused by a lapse of judgment that made them keep up the lies. These were their Achilles heel, and they would go to great lengths to keep it from those around them.

Sometimes a devastating event—a death, for instance—exposed the façade they had carefully cultivated for so long.

Was Reed hiding something he did not want anyone to know, not even his father? Rhodes could find nothing in his investigation that linked him to the barbershop or even the pizza shop.

Maybe Reed's death was a terrible accident. Maybe he was at the wrong place at the wrong time.

This reminded Rhodes of the case of the woman who was on her way to her friend's house when she decided to stop by a gas station. Even though there was more than enough gas in her car, she wanted to pump some more in case of an emergency. After filling up, she went inside to pay when an armed robber came in, demanding all the cash. The clerk behind the counter happened to be new, and in his eagerness, he tried to play the hero. Things didn't turn out as he had planned. Not only did the clerk get shot, but also an innocent bystander. The clerk somehow survived being shot in his stomach, but the woman who had come in to pay for gas died after being shot in her chest.

Rhodes believed what happened to the woman was a tragic accident. Had she not decided to stop for gas, she might have still been alive.

What if Reed had not lost his phone? More importantly, what if Reed had not gone to retrieve it? He surely would still be alive today.

Rhodes had a feeling there was more to this story than met the eye. He was determined to find out what it was.

SIXTY-SEVEN

Jo was at her desk when Chris came over. "You okay?" he asked. "You don't look so good."

Jo had her eyes closed and she was leaning back in her chair.

"I'm fine. I was just thinking."

"Actually, you know, I've been doing a lot of thinking too, lately."

Jo felt like her headache would turn into a full migraine. She was not in the mood to deal with Chris's quips and quirks right now.

"Is it about Irina?" Jo asked. "Because I still don't think she has changed her mind about going out with you."

"Really?" he asked. "I've been going out of my way to compliment her for the last couple of days. I've asked what diet she's on because she looks slimmer than before. I've inquired if she used to be a supermodel in Ukraine because she looks hot. I've even smelled her so I can tell her how much I like her perfume."

Jo raised an eyebrow. "She didn't punch you when you did that?"

"She has no idea. I always do it from behind her, and if she turns, I quickly make it look like I'm texting someone."

"Creepy," Jo finally said. She then added, "Is that why you are here, Chris?"

He squinted, shook his head and then said, "No, actually, I wanted to talk to you."

"Okay, what is it?" she said, rubbing her temples.

"I think we've been looking at this the wrong way."

"Looking at what?" she replied.

"We've been too focused on how the killer leaves the bodies on the trains…"

"So?" She was not sure where this was going, but she did not want to indulge Chris in another one of his wild theories.

"Don't you find it odd that we have recordings of him exiting the stations, but we have none showing him entering?"

Jo sat up straight.

Chris said, "We always assumed he came during the rush hour, or through a station with minimum surveillance. There are forty stations, you know. But what if he didn't?"

"What do you mean?"

"I mean, what if he didn't enter the stations through the main doors."

Jo stared at him.

He continued. "After this last victim, I had Walters contact BTA. It took a bit of pressure from her, but they sent me footage that they'd taken at all the stations that morning. I couldn't go through hours of footage from forty stations, so instead, I ran software that focused on individuals dressed in a jacket, hoodie, and baseball cap. These are the three items the killer had on when he exited the stations, so my search was very narrow and specific. And guess what I found?" Before Jo could say anything, he said, "No one matching the killer's description entered the station either through the turnstiles or even the revolving doors."

Jo was almost on the edge of her seat. "So, what are you saying? The killer entered some other way?"

"That's exactly what I'm saying," he said. "And I can prove it."

They walked over to Chris's desk. Once he was behind his computer, he pulled up a video. "This is from the first victim."

Jo watched as the killer carried Silvio Tarconi along the platform and stopped to wait for the train.

Chis said, "There are two cameras on either side of the platform, so both should catch what's happening there. I'll place the footage from each camera side by side. Just watch."

From the east camera, they saw the killer and Tarconi appear on the screen, but they were not on the west camera.

"How is that possible?" Jo asked, leaning closer to the screen. "There is only one exit on that platform, and the west camera should've caught whoever entered and exited the platform."

"That's what I was thinking too," Chris said. "It's like they magically appeared out of thin air."

"It *was* magic," Jo said.

Chris scrunched his face. "What? You really think so?"

"It's a magic trick. Do you know how magicians make people disappear in a box?"

"Sure. They have a hidden back door in the box."

"Exactly!" Jo exclaimed. "I'll bet my badge there is a maintenance door in the middle of that platform."

"What're you saying?" Chris asked.

"What I'm saying is the reason we haven't caught the killer entering any of the subway stations is because he's been entering them through BTA's underground tunnels."

SIXTY-EIGHT

Rhodes followed the Escalade all the way to a strip mall. He was not sure why Guzman was here. *Maybe he is going to visit his associates and gather ten grand*, Rhodes thought.

The Escalade drove past the front of the mall and swung into the back.

Rhodes debated whether he should do the same. It was one thing to follow the Escalade to the front of the mall—he could explain why he was there, by going to any of the stores—but it was another thing to follow the car around back. What would he say if he got caught?

He decided to take the risk. He could not afford to lose Guzman, not now.

Fortunately, there were other cars in the back of the mall. They most likely belonged to employees. In the distance, Rhodes spotted the Escalade. It was parked, but the engine was still running.

They are waiting for someone, Rhodes thought.

He found a parking spot and pulled into it.

He watched the Escalade. Fifteen minutes later, another vehicle entered the back of the mall. Rhodes spotted it in his rearview mirror.

The silver Audi drove past. Rhodes doubted the driver had spotted him.

The Audi parked in front of the Escalade. A man who barely looked twenty got out. He wore a flannel shirt, a sports jacket, khaki pants, and casual shoes.

Guzman and his bodyguard got out of the Escalade. They circled the man.

Rhodes was too far to hear them, but he could tell Guzman was agitated with the young man. He pointed and yelled at him.

The young man put his hands up in defense. Whatever he said, Guzman was not accepting it.

Guzman nodded to his bodyguard. He grabbed the young man by his shirt collar. The young man quickly stuffed his hands in his jacket pockets and pulled out what looked like money.

Guzman examined the money and became even more irate. He suddenly pulled out a gun and waved it at the man. His bodyguard pushed the man to his knees.

Are they going to execute him? Rhodes thought. *Should I get involved?*

Rhodes shook his head. *No, that would not be smart.*

The young man pleaded for his life, but Guzman began pacing back and forth. It looked like he was lecturing him.

Guzman stopped and pointed at the man's car. He said something and the young man shook his head. Guzman pressed his gun against the young man's temple. The young man began to cry. Guzman ordered him to stop.

The young man then pulled out his car keys and handed them to Guzman.

Guzman pointed the gun at the young man and said something to him. Rhodes could not tell what it was, but he was sure Guzman was warning the youth not to go to the police.

The bodyguard punched the young man in the face. He fell to the ground, covering his face. The bodyguard gave a roundhouse kick to the young man's stomach. He curled into a fetal position.

Guzman handed the keys to his bodyguard. The bodyguard got in the Audi while Guzman returned to the Escalade.

A few seconds later, both vehicles left the back of the mall.

Rhodes debated following them, but his instincts told him the young man was somehow involved in Reed's death. Plus, Rhodes already knew where Guzman and his bodyguard were heading. He could always catch up with them later.

He decided to follow the young man instead.

SIXTY-NINE

He took a sip of cognac. He had thick white hair with sharp gray eyes and leathery skin. He was in excellent shape for his age. He always had strong and sturdy hands, which came in handy in his line of work as a surgeon.

He took another sip and focused his attention on the television mounted on the wall of his residential office.

He could hear noises outside. It was his daughter's sixteenth birthday, and his wife had decided to throw her a surprise party in their five-thousand-square-foot home. He also had a daughter who was twelve. The older was more like her mother, outgoing and socially conscious. The youngest was more reserved and preferred small events rather than big ones, just like him.

He had wanted to get away from the party. The guests were mostly his wife's friends and acquaintances. He tried to be cordial with them, but he could not stand them. They always thought they were better than him. He did not know why. Like them, he came from wealth and privilege. But there was something different about him. He did not belong with them, and they knew it. But for the sake of his marriage, and for his daughters, he put up with them.

However, not all was bad. He had money, he had respect, and he had a family. What more could a man ask for?

It had taken him a long time to get to a place where he was comfortable, where he did not have to look over his shoulder. But somehow he could feel change happening in the air.

He always knew it could happen one day. Why wouldn't it when *he* was still alive? He should have gotten rid of him when he had the chance, but he did not. How would he have explained it to the world if he had? The focus would have turned on him, opening up old wounds.

No, what he did at that time was the right course of action. He just never expected things to turn out this way.

He watched as the reporter on the screen spoke about the Train Killings. She ended her segment by saying the FBI had no suspects or any leads at this time.

His face grew grim. He had a feeling, the longer this was allowed to happen, the more complicated his life was going to become.

There was a knock at the door. "Honey, are you coming down?" his wife said. "We're about to cut the cake."

"I'll be there in a sec," he replied.

He put his glass down, turned off the TV, and left.

SEVENTY

After speaking to Chris, Jo had called Walters and told her of their discovery. Walters had immediately convened a meeting where she, Jo, Tarik, Irina, Crowder, and Chris discussed their next course of action.

They understood why the killer had chosen to use the tunnels to enter the stations but not to exit. He did not want the authorities to know about the underground route. It was why he always chose to leave through the main doors of the stations. It was his way of throwing them off. If he left through the stations, the authorities would believe he must have also entered through them as well. The only reason he was doing it was because he wanted to keep using the tunnels to dump his victims' bodies.

That ends now, Jo vowed. *We will go down and bring him out.*

Chris had pulled up a map of the tunnels on a giant screen. It was then that they realized how massive the subway system was. It reminded Jo of a spider's web.

"He could be anywhere," Walters had said, staring at the screen.

Jo knew where to look. She told them, "Our focus will be on the stations the killer used to drop off the victims' bodies. We thought the killer had chosen those stations because they gave him a clean exit. We were wrong. He chose them because they are all close to each other. This means the killer kept the bodies somewhere in the vicinity of those stations in order to move the bodies through the tunnels and onto the platforms."

After the meeting, Irina and Tarik went to Davenport Station, Walters and another agent headed to Sherbourne Station, and Jo and Crowder had driven to Woodbine Station.

Crowder took the tunnel going east while Jo took the tunnel going west.

With a flashlight in one hand and her gun in the other, Jo walked carefully over the tracks. She had been advised by the BTA safety employee that the tracks contained 600 volts of live electricity.

There were lights on the tunnel ceiling, but they were not strong enough to see someone in the distance. There was no telling if the killer was still underground, though. Jo did not want him to get a jump on her. The tunnels had a foul odor, a stench that was the mixture of garbage and rotting flesh. Jo had seen rats the size of squirrels, and she assumed some of them had inadvertently made contact with the live tracks.

The first time she saw a rat, she had been so startled she almost fired her gun at the rodent.

She kept moving when she heard a noise coming toward her. She knew what it was. A train was heading in her direction.

As she had been instructed by the BTA employee, she got off the tracks and flattened her body next to the tunnel wall.

She waited when she saw bright lights round the bend. She closed her eyes and clenched her jaw as a train flew by her. She had to strain her body to stop from being sucked under the train.

She relaxed when the noise faded away.

She quickly got back on the tracks. She did not want to be caught by another train.

Jo moved down the tracks.

She stopped when something caught her attention. A strip of light was coming from somewhere down the tunnel.

She flashed her light and saw a door. She moved the light over it and caught the sign on the door: *MAINTENANCE.*

She placed the flashlight in her pocket and tightly gripped her weapon. She turned the doorknob with her free hand. It was unlocked.

She pushed the door in and entered with her gun aimed before her.

The room was small, no bigger than a car garage.

There was a table by the wall with a fluorescent light bulb hanging above it. She was moving toward it when her foot hit something. She looked down and saw a metal pail. There was liquid inside it. She looked carefully. The fluid was thick and red.

Blood.

She moved it to the table and found it was wet and sticky.

Fresh blood.

She suddenly realized where she was. She was in the killer's kill room.

She pulled out her cell phone, but found there was no signal. She was too deep underground.

She was about to put her phone away when something caught her eye. Another bucket was next to the table. The light was too low for her to see what was inside.

She pulled out her flashlight and shined it in the bucket. She quickly turned away to compose herself.

She flashed the light on the bucket again and found two hands, two eyes, and a tongue. They belonged to Silvio Tarconi, Natasha Wedham, and Doug Curran.

A putrid smell emanated from inside the bucket. She covered her nose with her hand.

She sensed a shadow behind her. She turned when something hard hit her in the spine. She fell forward and her head banged on the table. Her gun nearly flew out of her hands, but she held on to it.

She turned to fire a shot as the figure disappeared through the door.

She touched her forehead. It stung. There would be a bruise, but fortunately, there was no blood.

She got to her feet and ran after the figure.

SEVENTY-ONE

Rhodes watched as the young man waited at the bus stop. With his Audi taken, he could either walk from where he came from or take public transit. He took the latter.

The moment he got on the bus, Rhodes drove up right behind it. He was going to follow the bus to see where the young man got off. He wanted to find out who he was.

The bus kept going on its designated route, stopping only to drop off and pick up passengers.

When the bus finally turned into a station, Rhodes considered abandoning his chase. He could still catch up with Guzman. But then he thought, *I've come this far. I might as well keep going.*

After talking to Rhodes, Guzman had called the young man right away. Why? There had to be a reason. Did the young man merely owe drug money to Guzman? If so, this chase was a waste of time. Did the young man have anything to do with what happened to Reed? Rhodes was not sure, but the only way to find out was to not lose him.

He drove around for several minutes until he found a parking spot across from the station.

Rhodes raced up to the ticket booth and purchased a ticket. He went through the turnstiles and headed straight for the buses. He knew the bus number the young man had gotten on. As luck would have it, the bus was still at the station and people were still getting off.

He watched with bated breath until he spotted the young man. He had his head down, and he was clutching his stomach.

The young man followed the other passengers down the stairs on the other side of the station.

Rhodes ran and was down the stairs in no time. He saw the young man turn left at the end of the tunnel. *He is going east*, Rhodes thought.

Rhodes moved past a group of commuters and was at the end of the tunnel when he heard the sounds of a train.

He hurried his steps, but when he reached the platform, the train doors had already closed. The train slowly pulled out of the station.

Rhodes grunted. He had missed the train by mere seconds.

SEVENTY-TWO

Jo ran as fast as her legs would allow her, but she was careful not to touch the tracks. She heard footsteps up ahead. The killer was only a couple of yards away. If she could get in range, she was confident she could take him down with a bullet to the leg.

She heard the familiar sounds. A train was approaching from behind her.

She kept moving. She did not want to lose the killer. But when the sounds got louder, she gritted her teeth and shoved her body against the wall.

It did not take long for the train to speed past her.

She shut her eyes and held on tight. Her gun shook in her hand.

When the train was gone, she jumped back on the tracks and resumed her pursuit.

The tunnel swerved to the left. She followed it.

She saw a light in the distance. She also saw a figure running toward it.

She had not lost the killer!

But he was still too far for her to take a shot.

She was keeping pace when her breathing became heavier.

She felt disoriented.

A sharp pain stabbed her in the chest.

She broke into a cold sweat.

She grimaced as the pain overpowered her.

She tried to keep moving, but her legs became weak and wobbly.

Why is this happening? she thought. *Not now.*

She willed herself to keep going. She could no longer see the figure, but she could see light at the end of the tunnel.

By now, she was out of breath and heaving. If she could get to the next station, she could call it in.

Her legs gave way. Her body dropped to the ground. The flashlight fell out of her hand.

She lay in the middle of the track, her face inches from the rail. She stared at the ceiling. She was drenched in sweat. She tried to swallow, but her throat was dry.

The pain was throbbing inside her chest. She felt like her heart would explode.

She shut her eyes. She needed to compose herself. She needed to go after the killer.

She then felt vibrations underneath her.

She knew what was coming her way.

SEVENTY-THREE

Rhodes decided to head back to his car. There was nothing else he could do here. He looked at his watch. There was still time for him to be at the location before Guzman arrived.

He turned when he heard a noise. It sounded like footsteps. He listened carefully and realized it was coming from the tunnel.

Rhodes moved down the platform. He stuck his head out. It was dark inside the tunnel, but he could see a silhouette coming his way.

What the...?

Before he could react, a man jumped out and rammed into him, nearly knocking him off his feet.

Rhodes recovered, but the man was already racing up the stairs.

Odd, Rhodes thought.

He then noticed a light bouncing in the tunnel. He leaned over the platform to take a better look.

The light dropped to the floor and rolled away.

Something did not feel right, and his gut told him to check it out. He jumped on the track and moved into the tunnel, taking care to avoid the third rail. It was dark. The lights on the ceiling were not strong enough to illuminate his surroundings.

As he moved further into the tunnel, he saw a body on the ground. Next to it was a flashlight. He got closer and realized it was a woman. She had blonde hair, and she was gripping a gun.

Her eyes were open, and they were staring at him. He could tell she wanted to aim the gun at him, but something prevented her from doing so.

"I'm here to help," he said, stopping before her.

Just then, he heard the sound of the oncoming train.

He knew what to do next. He grabbed the woman, lifted her up on his shoulder, and ran as hard and fast as he could.

He felt a light behind him, but he did not bother to turn and see what it was. He already knew. The sound of the train was loud and deafening.

He reached the platform, threw the woman on it and then pulled himself up.

Just then, he felt a strong gust of wind behind him as the train roared into the station.

He looked over at the woman. Her eyes were open but she was pale.

A disembarking passenger came over. "She okay?" he asked.

"Get some water," Rhodes replied.

SEVENTY-FOUR

Jo had refused to go to the hospital even though Walters insisted on it. "You need medical attention," she said.

"I'm fine."

"What happened on the tracks?"

Jo looked away.

"Did it have anything to do with your condition?" Walters asked.

"The killer got a jump on me." Jo pointed to the bruise on her forehead. "I ran so fast after him that I may have gotten disoriented."

"It's a good thing he pulled you out." Walters looked over at a man who was standing in the corner. "Who knows what could've happened if he didn't."

Jo did not say anything.

Walters put her hand on her shoulders. "The FBI can't afford to lose one of their own. *I* can't afford to lose a member of my team."

Jo nodded. She knew that beneath her hard exterior, Walters cared deeply for those who reported to her. She also knew how concerned Walters was for her health.

Jo then said, "I was in the kill room. I saw where he cut up his victims. You'll find all three victims appendages in that room."

"I've spoken to BTA, and they'll be rerouting all trains away from that tunnel. I'm going to have a team go through that room with a fine comb. Did you see what he looked like?"

Jo shook her head. "It happened too fast. What did he say, though?" She nodded at the man who had pulled her out of the tunnel. He was looking impatient as if he was in a hurry to be somewhere.

"He didn't say much," Walters replied. "Only that a man ran out of the tunnel in a hurry and that you were behind him."

Jo was relieved. Maybe he did not see her clutching her chest when she fell to the ground. Why would he, though? She was too far from the platform.

"He did say that if it weren't for your flashlight, he wouldn't have known someone was on the tracks. You were lucky."

In more ways than one, Jo thought. She was lucky that the man had seen her light. She was even luckier that he risked his life to save her.

Walters said, "Do you know who that is, though?"

Jo shrugged.

"Martin Rhodes."

Jo squinted. "Why does that name sound familiar?"

"It should. He used to be a detective in Newport."

"Used to be?"

"Yes, until he shot and killed a suspect?"

"A suspect?" Jo asked, trying to recall the case.

"Yes, and that suspect turned out to be a child murderer."

"I remember now. He spent ten years in prison for it." Jo stared at the man. If it were not for him, she would not be standing here now.

Walters said, "I don't know what he's doing in Bridgeton. I hope he doesn't plan to stay here too long. I can't stand police officers who take the law into their own hands."

A paramedic walked over to them.

Walters said, "If you won't go to the hospital, then at least let these guys check you out."

Jo conceded.

The paramedic put his bag next to her. He quickly pulled out his equipment. He first checked her forehead and then he flashed a light in her eyes. He pulled out his stethoscope and began to check her heart. Jo could tell Walters must have said something to him.

By the time the examination was done, Martin Rhodes was gone.

SEVENTY-FIVE

Rhodes came out of the station and found his car missing.

He walked around the block, hoping he might have parked it somewhere else, but there was no sign of it.

"It might've been towed," he heard a voice say.

He turned and found it was the same woman he had pulled out of the tunnel.

"It happens sometimes," she said. "If you park in the wrong spot, they won't even bother giving you a ticket, they just haul it away."

A man with a guitar approached them. He looked like a street performer. "Are you the owner of the Malibu?"

Rhodes nodded.

"I was playing music over there," he said, pointing at a spot across the street, "and I saw a man run out of the station. He saw your car and jumped in and drove away."

"Can you describe the man?" Jo said.

The man shrugged. "I guess so. I didn't get a good look at his face, but he was wearing a jacket and a baseball cap."

"That's my suspect," Jo said. She turned to Rhodes. "What's your license plate number?"

Rhodes gave it to her.

Jo pulled out her cell phone and called Chris. She told him to send out an all-points-bulletin to all law enforcement agencies.

She hung up. "If he's still driving that car, we'll grab him."

The witness said to Rhodes, "You shouldn't keep your windows down. You're asking someone to take it, you know."

Rhodes looked at him. He was certain the windows were up and that the car was locked. Maybe in his haste, he had been negligent.

Rhodes looked at his watch. *Shit*, he thought. Guzman would be at the location by now. The day was not turning out the way he had planned it.

"You need to be somewhere?" the woman asked.

Rhodes nodded.

"I can drive you."

He looked at her.

"It's the least I can do. You saved my life."

He thought about it. "I should get home, but I need to make a call first."

"You can use my phone." She offered it to him.

Rhodes was not sure he wanted her involved. "I prefer to use the phone booth. It's a private call."

They were silent at first during the drive, but Jo finally broke the ice, "By the way, I'm Jo."

"Martin," Rhodes replied.

"I know. My supervisor told me," she said. She paused and then added, "She also told me you used to be a detective."

Rhodes said nothing. He just stared out the window.

"I can tell you're not much of a talker," she said.

He did not say anything.

"Why were you chasing that man?" Rhodes asked her.

"We think he's responsible for the death of three people."

"Do you mean the bodies on the train?"

"Yes."

Rhodes nodded as if it now made more sense.

She said, "I had found the room where he had butchered the bodies, and that's when he jumped me."

Rhodes turned to her. "And you chased him until he jumped you *again* on the train tracks?"

So he knows what happened, she thought. She looked away.

"I won't tell anyone," he said. "It's none of my business."

Jo gripped the steering wheel. "I have a medical condition," she confessed. She was not sure why she was telling him, but it felt like a relief to share it with someone. She had been carrying it inside her for so long that the weight was worse than the actual condition. Plus, if he had wanted to out her secret, he would have already done so. "My condition got worse with all the excitement and stress, but it'll be fine." She was trying to reassure herself more than him.

"In our line of work... I mean, in *your* line of work, something like this can get you killed," Rhodes replied.

"I know," Jo said.

They drove in silence for a time.

"Thanks," Jo said.

He nodded and went back to staring out the window.

SEVENTY-SIX

Crowder had received a call. It had come from a pay phone. Crowder thought it was someone trying to play a prank on him. But what the caller told him made him think it might be something he should look into.

He was now in the interview room at the police station. The room had a two-way mirror. Two men watched eagerly from behind it.

The suspect's name was Alfonso Guzman. Crowder had picked up him and his buddy outside a bar.

"Why am I here?" Guzman asked, sitting on a chair.

"We received a tip," Crowder said, circling him.

"What're you talking about? What tip?"

"That you were involved in the death of Reed Yates."

Guzman made a face. "Who's that? I don't know that name. Whoever called you, they lied to you, man."

"Well, the caller told us where to find you. We did. The caller said you would be armed. You were. The caller also said that you would be carrying lots of cash. You had in your possession close to six thousand dollars."

Guzman went silent.

Crowder continued, "The caller said that you had beaten him up and had taken his car at gunpoint. Is that true?"

The blood drained on Guzman's face.

Crowder smiled. "I'm guessing you know who I'm talking about."

"That rat," Guzman spat. "He's a dead man."

"I wouldn't say that at a police station," Crowder said. "But I'll get to him later. What I want to know is how you are involved in Reed Yates's death?"

Guzman crossed his arms over his chest. "I want my lawyer."

"Sure, you have the right to an attorney, but before you make that call, just remember that once your lawyer is here, I won't show you any leniency. Right now, if you answer my questions, it might not be *all* bad for you."

Guzman did not look convinced.

"Plus, we have seized your gun, which we checked and found it was not registered, so that's a felony in this city. On top of that, I'm thinking if we did ballistics tests on it, we might find a match from your gun to the bullet found in Reed Yates's body. What do you think?"

Guzman swallowed. He stared at Crowder and shook his head. "Shit," he said. "I didn't mean to shoot him, okay? The guy was being unreasonable. He wanted to take *my* phone."

"Your phone?" Crowder said.

"Yeah, I told him I had bought it."

"From who?"

"The same guy who ratted me out."

"What's his name?"

"I don't know his full name, but he was white."

"Did he at least have a first name?"

"Derek, I think."

"How did he know Reed Yates?"

Guzman shrugged. "I think he was the guy's best friend or something. He said he took the guy's phone from his school locker."

"And why did this Derek give you the phone?" Crowder asked.

"He didn't give it to me. He sold it to me."

"For how much?"

Guzman shook his head. "It doesn't work like that."

"What doesn't?"

Guzman went silent.

"Come on, talk to me," Crowder said. "What you have to tell me can't be worse than going to prison for murder."

Guzman sighed. "He gave me the phone in exchange for some goods I had sold him."

"You mean drugs."

Guzman licked his lips and nodded.

Crowder said, "Just so that I understand, the phone was a payment for the drugs you had given to this Derek person, is that right?"

"Yeah, that's right."

Crowder looked over at the mirror and then continued. "Okay, so Derek gave you the phone and then Reed Yates later showed up to get his phone back, but why shoot him? It was only a phone."

Guzman put his palms on the table. "Like I told you before, it was an accident."

"Please explain that to me, because right now I don't get it."

"I thought he was gonna shoot me."

Crowder leaned forward. "What?"

"Yeah, I told the guy to beat it. It was my phone. But he insisted it was his. He said he had a GPS tracker on it and that's how he found me. The guy was persistent. I pulled out my gun. I didn't mean to shoot him. I just wanted to scare him, you know."

"But you did shoot him."

Guzman looked away.

"Alfonso," Crowder said. "You shot Reed Yates, didn't you?"

"I want my lawyer."

Crowder stared at him and then said, "Fine. We'll play it your way. But the moment I leave this room, I won't be able to help you."

Guzman put his face in his hands. "I thought he was gonna shoot me."

"Reed Yates, you mean?"

"Yeah. He reached inside his jacket and I thought he was gonna pull out a gun, but…"

"But what?"

Guzman went silent.

"But what, Alfonso?"

Guzman's shoulders sagged. "It wasn't a gun."

"What was it?"

"It was an inhaler."

"For asthma?"

"I guess so. I didn't mean to. It was an accident."

Guzman broke down.

Crowder left the room and entered the room adjacent to it. Chief Baker and Tim Yates had seen the entire confession.

"We got our man," Crowder said.

Yates turned to the chief. "Thank you for allowing me to observe this."

"You're welcome, and I hope the PD won't be hearing from your lawyer anymore."

"Absolutely," Yates said. "And, thank you again."

As Yates was leaving, the chief added, "In cases like these, anything can change the course of an investigation. This doesn't mean we aren't doing our jobs. We are sometimes one anonymous tip away from solving a case."

Yates knew the tip was not anonymous. It was Martin Rhodes.

SEVENTY-SEVEN

The car pulled into the back of the house. Rhodes got out. "Thanks for the ride," he said.

"No problem," Jo replied.

Rhodes walked up to his apartment. He saw Tess's mom waiting by his front door.

"Where is she?" the mom said.

"Where is who?" he replied.

"Tess."

"How would I know?" he asked, confused.

"I saw her sitting in your car earlier."

Rhodes's heart sank.

Rhodes turned and ran back to Jo, who was pulling her car out of the back lane. He waved to her. She stopped.

He leaned over to her window. "We need to find my car."

"I've put a call out already," she replied.

"You don't understand. A neighbor of mine might be in that car."

Jo was confused. "What…?"

"I'll explain later, but we have to find it."

"Okay, get in."

As they drove, Rhodes told her about Tess and how she had once hidden in his trunk.

"How can you be sure she was in the car today?"

"The window," Rhodes replied. "The witness outside the station mentioned my window was down. I thought that didn't make sense, but now it does. Tess must have rolled it down."

"What if she wasn't there when the killer took it?" Jo suggested.

"If that was the case, then she would've come home by now," he said.

Rhodes frowned. He now regretted letting her use his car as a refuge from her problems at home. He should have let her sit on his front steps when he had first met her. At least then her life would not be in danger.

SEVENTY-EIGHT

Tess gripped the handrest as the man drove erratically around the city.

Earlier, when Rhodes had parked the car by the subway station, Tess had used the backseat to get out of the trunk.

She wanted to surprise him.

She knew he would be upset with her, but she wanted to be part of his investigation. She wanted to help him solve the case he was working on. It was more exciting than sitting outside her house, waiting for her mom's creepy boyfriend to leave.

Helping Rhodes at the pizza shop made her feel needed. She never knew her dad, and her mom moved from one job to another, one city to another, and one boyfriend to another. Throughout all this, she was nothing more than someone who tagged along with her mother.

There were times when she felt like her mom would have been happier if she was never born. Her mom never said it, but she felt it.

She did not think anyone cared for her or protected her, not even her mom. Her mom did not even take her side when it came to her boyfriend. She accused Tess of lying. She thought Tess was jealous that she finally had someone in her life.

That was not the case. Tess wanted her mom to be happy. She wanted someone to take care of her mom like she wanted her mom to take care of her. But more often than not, Tess felt like she was on her own.

With Rhodes, it was somehow different. He had tried to ignore her, but she could tell he cared. He did not have to stick his nose in when it came to her mom and boyfriend, but he did. Ever since he had, her life had been a little easier.

When Rhodes had parked at the station and left, she had decided to come out of her hiding place. She waited for him in the passenger seat. But the car became hot and she decided to roll down the windows. That's when this guy jumped in the car. She was going to scream, but he showed her a knife and told her to keep her mouth shut.

He asked for the car keys. Her eyes flicked up at the driver's side visor. She had seen Rhodes keep an extra set of keys there.

She begged the man to let her go and just take the car, but he did not listen to her. He drove off in a hurry.

As the Malibu weaved in and out of traffic, she said, "Please let me go."

"I can't," the man replied.

"You can drop me off by the side of the road."

"You saw my face," he said.

"I won't tell anyone, I promise."

"Just shut up and let me think."

SEVENTY-NINE

Jacopo was furious at himself. His knuckles were white as he gripped the steering wheel tight. He could not believe they had found his kill room.

How was that possible? His master had planned everything with incredible skill, and he had executed the plans to perfection.

Then what went wrong? he thought.

He tried to go over all his steps, but he could not see where he had slipped up.

Maybe I shouldn't have gone back into the tunnel, he thought. *Maybe I should've cleaned up before I dumped the last body.*

He gritted his teeth. *I got careless*, he told himself.

He should have dumped his victim's appendages when he had the chance. Instead, he kept them in a bucket, as if they were trophies of his kill.

He had gotten cocky. He thought he could clean up his mess later. He thought he had time. The police were too far in their pursuit, he believed. The news reporter was their way of keeping a tab on the FBI. She always reported on their progress on the case.

He should have known something was wrong when she had failed to report anything new. The FBI had withheld vital information from the media. This should have raised a red flag, but it was not his job to monitor this, it was his master's.

Jacopo shook his head.

He could not blame his master. That would be wrong. It was not his master who had failed. It was him.

His master had always told him to leave no evidence behind. He did. He was going to dump the bucket of appendages at a more convenient time.

His master had told him to always wear gloves. He did not. He found it was easier to perform the procedures with his bare hands.

Now the entire kill room was covered in his fingerprints.

"Shit!"

He pounded on the steering wheel.

The girl next to him, let out a scream.

He turned to her. She instantly fell silent when she saw the look on his face.

He should not have brought her with him, but he needed a hostage in case things got complicated.

He would kill her and dump her body when the time suited him, but for now, he had to find a way to contact his master.

EIGHTY

Rhodes felt helpless.

They were driving back to the spot where his car was taken from, but he knew it was a waste of time. Agent Pullinger—Jo, as she had corrected him many times now—was on the phone throughout. She had contacted every law enforcement agency in Bridgeton. She was doing her utmost to locate his Chevy Malibu, and ultimately, Tess.

Rhodes wanted to do something. But what could he do that the FBI was not?

If anything happened to Tess, he was not sure if he could forgive himself. There was already too much blood on his hands. He could not bear any more of it.

Tess was innocent in every sense of the word. She had harmed nobody. In fact, there were others out there who wanted to harm her, and he did not just mean the killer. The killer had used an opportunity to his advantage. He was escaping capture, and when he saw an unlocked vehicle, he did not hesitate to make use of it.

Rhodes was thinking of her mother. She had neglected Tess, which was why she had looked for a father figure from a total stranger. Rhodes was nothing more than that to her, he believed.

Rhodes had never been a father to anyone, and he had no desire to be one in the future. Tess was a good kid, and he felt bad for her. He meant every word when he had warned her mother and her creepy boyfriend about treating Tess improperly. Rhodes would have made good on his promise if anything remotely bad happened to her.

Why? Why am I getting involved in something that does not concern me?

Maybe it had something to do with his upbringing. Tess did not know her father, and Rhodes would have been better off if he did not know his father either. At least Rhodes had had a loving and caring mother. Tess did not even have that.

Maybe that was why he felt this anger inside him now. It was consuming him, eating away at every fiber in him. He had not felt this way since he had shot and killed that man almost ten years ago. If the man who had taken Tess was standing in front of him now, would Rhodes do the same to him? Shoot him without a second thought?

He was grateful he did not own a weapon. He no longer trusted himself with one.

Jo's phone rang again, and he turned to her eagerly.

Jo listened and said to him, "Unfortunately, we still have not located your vehicle, but my supervisor spoke to BTA security, and they know who the killer is. His name is Craig Orton. He was a former BTA employee. Several years ago, Craig Orton drove a bus full of passengers into a lamp post. Fortunately, no one was seriously injured. But when he was taken in for questioning, they found Craig Orton was under the influence of drugs and alcohol. At the time of the accident, Orton's marriage had fallen apart, and he was fighting his ex for the custody of his daughter. Prior to this, there were other incidents involving him. He had once assaulted a passenger who had been rude to him. He also had issues with his superiors regarding his tardiness and erratic behavior. Unsurprisingly, after the incident with the bus, the BTA fired him. His union couldn't help him either because he'd had too many strikes against him. This explains why he was using the subway to dump his victims."

Rhodes thought of something. "I'm not too familiar with the Train Killer case, but weren't the victims from some mental institute?"

"They were," Jo agreed. "And, apparently, right after the bus incident, he was referred to the Bridgeton Mental Care Institute."

Rhodes thought about it and nodded. He then looked out the window. The feeling of powerlessness did not leave him. In fact, he felt even worse after what he had heard. Craig Orton was not only a murderer but also insane.

Sensing his mood, Jo said, "We will find him. And we will find your neighbor. I promise."

Rhodes did not respond. He just stared out at the passing streets.

EIGHTY-ONE

Jacopo was breathing heavily. He tried to control his composure, but nothing worked.

He needed his master now more than ever. He just was not sure how to contact him.

His master came to him, not vice versa. His master always chose the time and place, and he always kept himself hidden from him. Jacopo always thought this was odd. Did his master not trust him enough to reveal his true identity? Jacopo trusted his master implicitly, and he wished his master would trust him in return.

Maybe his master was waiting for the time when he had truly proved himself. Maybe he was waiting for when the mission was complete.

Jacopo grimaced. His carelessness had nearly sabotaged the mission. Now he was not sure if his master would ever reveal himself to him.

He took a deep breath.

Not all was lost. The FBI agent had not gotten a good look at his face. He had gotten a jump on her before she had the chance. On top of that, the tunnel was too dark for her to see clearly.

His heart sank again.

The FBI was probably going through his kill room with a fine toothcomb. He did not have time to scrub it clean. They would surely find something that would connect him to the murders.

He punched the steering wheel.

The girl jumped up from her seat. He had startled her.

He had forgotten she was there. She was another problem he had to deal with.

He had his knife in his pocket. He could cut her throat and dump her body by the side of the road.

He had already committed three murders. What was one more?

Yes, that's what he would do. Stab her in the chest with the knife and then bleed her until she was gone.

But a thought popped in his head. He could not do it in a moving car. Plus, it would be messy. The blood would easily get on him. He still had to go back to his luxury apartment and retrieve his belongings. How would he explain the blood if anyone saw him?

Another thought came to him. What if the FBI was already at his apartment?

He cursed.

He could not go back.

It was too risky.

He felt like a caged animal with nowhere to run. The FBI was closing in on him. And he was running out of options.

He suddenly had an idea.

He turned the wheel and drove in the other direction.

EIGHTY-TWO

Tess thought about jumping out of the car, but at the speed they were going, she knew she would either seriously hurt herself, or worse, she would not survive the fall. Plus, there were cars right behind her coming at a fast pace.

She had to come up with a plan.

She was not sure if anyone knew she was with this man, so it was up to her to do something. There was no telling what this man would do to her once he stopped the car. On numerous occasions, he had moved his hand over the side pocket of his jacket. It was where she had seen him keep his knife.

She did not believe for one bit that he would let her go. She knew what he looked like. She had watched too much television and seen too many movies to know that he would kill her the moment he got the chance.

She could not let that happen.

He was too strong for her to overpower him. Even he knew that which was why he had not restrained her yet.

But she was smarter than him.

She leaned back and gently pulled out her cell phone from her back pocket.

She thought about calling her mom, but dialing her would mean punching a lot of numbers, or scrolling for her name in her contact list.

She looked over at the man.

He was mumbling and preoccupied with his driving.

She slowly and carefully dialed 9-1-1.

EIGHTY-THREE

Jo received another call. She answered and then put it on speaker phone.

"Someone just called 9-1-1," Chris said. "They are in a moving vehicle. I've traced the signal and it's only two miles away. If you take the next exit, you will be right behind them."

Jo looked over at Rhodes.

"It's Tess," he said with conviction.

Jo nodded and swung the car around.

The Jetta zoomed past several cars as it hit over a hundred miles an hour. Fortunately, the highway was not busy.

They would reach the car in no time.

EIGHTY-FOUR

Everything would be alright, Jacopo thought.

He would start a new life somewhere else. His master had given him enough money for him to disappear forever. He would not stay in the United States. No. He would go to countries where they could not extradite him. He was not sure which countries they were, but they would be easy to find on the internet.

After making a quick stop, he would kill the girl and burn her body in the car. By the time the FBI would piece everything together, he would be long gone.

He was proud of himself for having a contingency plan. It was something he had learned from his master. His master, it seemed, was always thinking a step ahead of everyone. It was why the FBI or the local police were unable to stop him thus far. It was his master who had told him to wear a baseball cap and a hoodie. It was his master who had told him to never look up at the security cameras. More importantly, it was his master who had told him where to park outside the subway stations. He knew all the hidden CCTV camera spots in the city.

His master had planned everything down to the last detail.

He, Jacopo, would do the same.

He turned and smiled at the girl. That's when he noticed her body was shielding her right hand.

"What do you have there?" he yelled.

She did not respond.

"Show me or else I will throw you out of the car," he growled.

She held out her cell phone.

It was on, and it was dialed to 9-1-1.

He snatched it from her and threw it out the window.

He slapped her across the head. She covered her face.

"You pull any more stunts like that," he said, pointing a finger at her. "I will remove your hands, your eyes, and your tongue. You will never be able to tell anyone who I am. Got it?"

She was crying.

"Do you understand me?!" he screamed.

She nodded between tears.

He turned back to the road. He scowled. He should cut her up right now and let her live. It would be a cruel but fitting punishment for what she just did.

He would get to her soon, though. In the meantime, he had some unfinished business.

EIGHTY-FIVE

"The signal has stopped moving," Chris said over the speaker phone.

"Where is it?" Jo asked.

"You'll reach it in two minutes."

They were still on the highway, and there was a lot of traffic by then.

Jo was not sure why the killer would choose to stop his car there.

She dreaded the worst.

Rhodes stuck his head out the window.

"I see something," he said. "Stop the car."

Jo slowed the Jetta and turned on the hazard lights.

A few cars honked behind her, but she pulled the vehicle to the side of the road.

Rhodes jumped out and ran a few feet from the car.

He returned with a cell phone.

His face was ashen. "It's Tess's," he said.

"What do we do now?" Jo said.

He did not respond. He kept staring at the phone.

"Where does this highway go?" he asked.

"What do you mean?"

"I mean, why would Craig Orton be on it? Where was he going?"

Jo understood. She turned to the speaker phone. "Chris, can you check to see if anyone related to Craig Orton lives nearby."

They heard Chris tap on his keyboard.

"Oh, wow," Chris finally said.

"What?" Jo asked.
"You wouldn't believe this, but Orton's ex-wife and daughter live only a mile away."

EIGHTY-SIX

When the woman opened the door, her eyes widened with shock. "Craig, what are you doing here?" she asked. She had dirty blond hair, green eyes, and a pale complexion.

"I need to see Ally," he replied.

"You're not allowed to come near us. Have you forgotten there is a restraining order against you?"

"I know, but I have to see Ally now."

His ex-wife did not move away from the door. "Leave right now, Craig, or else I am calling the police."

He pulled out a gun and aimed it at her stomach.

She froze and then slowly moved back. He entered.

"Who is she?" His ex-wife asked once she saw a girl with him. The girl looked scared. It looked like she had been crying.

"Don't worry about her." They moved to the living room. "Sit down," he ordered the girl. She did.

"Where is Ally?" he said, turning to his ex-wife.

"Don't do anything stupid, Craig," his ex-wife warned him. "If you leave now, I won't call the police."

His hand shot out and grabbed her throat. He placed the gun to her forehead. "You will *not* threaten me, not anymore, do you understand?"

She was terrified. She nodded.

"Now, I'm going to ask you again, where is Ally?"

"She's... she's upstairs in her room."

"Call her."

His ex-wife hesitated.

"If you don't, I will put a bullet in your head. And then I'll take Ally and disappear."

She swallowed. "Ally, baby, please come downstairs," she said.

There were footsteps on the second floor.

"Don't try to do anything stupid, do you understand?" he warned her.

She nodded.

He released her and put the gun away.

Just then, a girl, not even five, with blonde hair, blue eyes, and wearing a polka dot dress, came down the stairs.

"Hey baby," he said with a smile. "Look who's here? Your daddy."

The girl hesitated and looked over at her mother.

"It's okay, Ally," her mother assured her.

The girl reluctantly walked over to him.

He put his arms around her and hugged her.

"I missed you so much," he said.

The girl did not hug him back. She stood still.

"How are you?" he asked.

"I'm okay, I guess."

"Good. Did you miss your daddy?" he asked.

She looked over at her mother. She told her to say yes.

"Yes, I did," the girl replied.

He looked his daughter in the eyes. "After today, baby, everything will be alright. I promise."

EIGHTY-SEVEN

"Craig, please leave us alone," his ex-wife said. "I promise, I won't call the police."

"I want to trust you, but I can't," he shot back. "The moment I'm out the door, the cops will be waiting for me around the corner."

"Don't hurt Ally," his ex-wife pleaded.

He grimaced. "I would *never* hurt my daughter," he said, offended that she would even think this.

"What do you want from us?" she said.

He began pacing back and forth. "I don't know... wait, I know... all I wanted from day one was for us to be a family again. I know I drank a lot, and sometimes I got angry, but I loved you and Ally."

"You were abusive."

"I'm sorry," he said. "I didn't mean to, but I'm better now. I haven't had a drink in years, and I have money... I have a lot of money."

"Did you steal it?" she asked.

"Of course not. My master gave it to me."

She looked confused. "What're you talking about?"

"I can't go into any details, but I want you and Ally to come with me. Together we'll go somewhere far. How about South America? We used to talk about moving there before."

"That was a long time ago when we were still married. It's over between us now, Craig."

"It's not!" he said. His eyes blazed with anger.

"Craig, you need help. I can get you help."

He felt a migraine coming on. "I want my family back."

"You can't. It's over. You have to move on."

He frowned and pulled out his gun.

She froze.

"You have to promise me, you and Ally will stay with me."

His ex-wife reached out and grabbed her daughter. She held her close to her. His ex-wife had tears in her eyes. "I'm sorry, Craig. We can't be with you, not now, not ever."

"Then, I'm sorry too."

He held out the gun and aimed.

Suddenly, a shadow passed the window.

He turned to his ex-wife. "Did you call the police?"

She shook her head.

He turned to his hostage. "I know *you* did."

He pointed the gun at the ceiling and fired. They all screamed. Plaster and debris fell to the floor.

He moved to the window and yelled, "I know you are outside. Drop your weapon and come in with your arms up. If you don't, I'll shoot everyone in the house. And then I'll shoot myself. Do you understand?"

A few seconds later, a female voice replied, "Yes, I do."

He walked over and carefully unlocked the front door.

He held it open. A woman entered with her hands up.

He looked outside but saw no one.

"I'm alone," the woman said.

He checked her holster. It was empty.

"Sit down next to them," he ordered.

He then pointed the gun at her head.

EIGHTY-EIGHT

"It's over, Mr. Orton," Jo said. "The police are on their way. They will surround this house in a matter of minutes."

"Shut up!" he said.

"There is no way out."

"I said shut up!"

He kept the gun aimed at her.

"You don't want to hurt anyone, especially not your daughter."

He looked at his daughter and his eyes welled up. "It wasn't supposed to be like this," he mumbled. "We were supposed to be one happy family."

"Drop the gun," Jo insisted. "Let us end this peacefully."

He paced back and forth, muttering to himself, pounding his feet on the hardwood floor. He stopped and turned to face them. His face was grim.

He took a step back toward the front windows and cocked the gun.

"I'm sorry," he said.

"Don't do this," Jo replied.

"I don't have much choice."

Something smashed the window. He looked down and saw it was a piece of brick.

Before he could react, a hand shot out through the broken pane and grabbed him around the neck.

He tried to break free, but his assailant was too strong and powerful.

He pulled him through the window.

Glass cut him as he fell onto the porch.

He turned and saw it was the same man he had seen on the train platform.

The man swung his fist, slamming Jacopo in his cheek.

He was disoriented, but he held on to the gun.

The man swung again, but he blocked it with his knee.

He kicked the man in the chin.

The man stumbled back, but then he was back on his feet in an instant.

He aimed the gun at the man's chest.

Before he could pull the trigger, his body shook.

He looked down and saw blood on his shirt.

What the hell…?

He turned and saw through the broken window that the woman had a gun aimed directly at him.

He cursed and lifted his gun at her.

She fired. Several bullets penetrated his body, shaking it like a rag doll.

He fell to the ground with a loud thud.

His last thought was of his master and how he had failed him.

EIGHTY-NINE

Jo was glad they had ended the Train Killings. The killer was dead, and there would be no more dead bodies.

She was also glad the Rhodes's neighbor was safe. She was tough, and Jo knew she would overcome this ordeal. If it were not for her 9-1-1 call, they would not have been able to find her and Craig Orton.

Orton's wife and daughter were also relieved that they did not have to worry about him terrorizing them anymore.

His death had eased a lot of lives.

Rhodes had thanked Jo for her help, but she felt like it was she who should have been thanking him. After all, if it were not for him, she would not be alive.

She had offered to give Rhodes and his neighbor a ride, but they declined. They had plans of their own.

Jo had called Walters and told her about what had happened at the house. Walters then told her something that shook her to the core.

The name Orton had used to lease the condo and rent the Mercedes was none other than Dagmar Kole.

Kole was thought to have been the Bridgeton Ripper, and her father's killer. He was eventually exonerated. But why had Orton used his name? Jo wasn't sure.

At the moment, though, she did not care.

She took a deep breath and touched her chest.

Her heart could only take so much excitement in one day.

Maybe it is time I took that vacation, she thought.

NINETY

Jo knocked on the door. Her sister-in-law opened it.

"Hey there, stranger," Kim said with a big smile. "Where have you been?"

Before Jo could respond, she heard a girl squeal, "Aunty Jo!"

Her niece ran over and gave Jo a big hug. Jo held on to her. It felt nice and warm.

"Aunty Jo, where were you?" Chrissy asked.

"I was busy," Jo replied.

"You were catching bad guys?"

"Yes, I was."

"I'm going to catch bad guys too when I grow up."

Her brother came over. He looked horrified by what his daughter had just said. Jo knew Sam had already lost a father to the profession, and he feared he would one day lose his sister to it as well.

Jo said to Chrissy, "Your dad catches bad guys too."

"He does?"

"Yep, and he catches the big and scary bad guys. They take other people's money, and they hurt more people."

"Wow." Her eyes widened. "I want to be like daddy."

Chrissy went over and hugged her dad.

Sam smiled. "Okay, now let's have dinner."

Kim brought out a pot roast while Jo helped Sam set up the table.

They laughed and ate, and for a brief moment, Jo had no worries in the world. Her failing heart, searching for her father's killer, solving more crimes—nothing mattered to her at that moment. What mattered was that she was with her family.

NINETY-ONE

Tim Yates paid Rhodes the money he was owed. He wanted to give him extra, but Rhodes declined. According to him, a deal was a deal.

Rhodes then headed straight to the House of Hope. He took Tess along with him to the homeless shelter.

There was already a line outside the shelter, but Rhodes managed to get in after asking for Father Mike.

He handed him a thick envelope.

Father Mike looked inside and said, "That's a lot of money."

"Please take it. You can do more good with it than I can. Plus, without your help, I'd probably have slept on the streets on my first night in the city."

Father Mike was still in shock. "Thank you from the bottom of my heart. Do you guys want to join us for dinner? We could use a hand."

Rhodes looked over at Tess. She was smiling.

"Sure," he said.

Tess grabbed paper plates and plastic cutlery and began setting up the tables.

Once all the tables were set, Tess turned to Rhodes, "Thanks again for coming for me."

"Why wouldn't I?" he replied.

She shrugged. "Maybe because you'd be happy no one would bother you anymore."

"That's true," he said. "But then who would help me solve my cases."

Her face brightened. "Really? You'll let me be your partner?"

"I never said that," Rhodes replied. "All I'm saying is that I might need someone who knows the streets of Bridgeton more than I do."

She was smiling from ear to ear. "Will I get paid?"

Rhodes raised an eyebrow. "We'll talk salary later."

They served food to over fifty people. Then Rhodes and Tess joined the homeless, the destitute, and the forgotten people of Bridgeton for dinner.

There was nowhere else Rhodes would have rather been than with them.

A FEW DAYS LATER

Ellen left BN-24's headquarters and stormed to the parking lot. Ever since the FBI killed the man responsible for the Train Killings, Ellen's position was back to where it was prior to the murders.

Dan Ferguson had decided to return to work full-time, and Miles was more than willing to give some of her stories to him. Ellen knew he was punishing her for not telling him about her contact with the killer.

She wanted to say to him, *why would I tell you when you don't take me seriously?* What he was doing to her now was exactly what he did to her before.

Without her and her exclusive story, BN-24 would not have been the most-watched news channel in the city. They had even beaten out Janie Fernandez and SUNTV for the top spot.

Janie.

She was back to her old tricks. She was using her charm and beauty to win back all the viewers she had lost. Ellen despised her even more.

No matter. She would find a way to get back on top.

The world could not keep Ellen Sheehan down for long.

The world was spinning with stories, and she would once again take one and use it to her advantage.

She unlocked her car door and got in.

She was putting her key in the ignition when she felt something cold on the back of her neck.

She looked up at the rearview mirror.

She was about to say something when a bullet ripped through her skull, splattering blood and brains onto the windshield.

Visit the author's website:
www.finchambooks.com

Contact:
finchambooks@gmail.com

Join my Facebook page:
https://www.facebook.com/finchambooks/

MARTIN RHODES

1) Close Your Eyes
2) Cross Your Heart
3) Say Your Prayers
4) Fear Your Enemy

THOMAS FINCHAM holds a graduate degree in Economics. His travels throughout the world have given him an appreciation for other cultures and beliefs. He has lived in Africa, Asia, and North America. An avid reader of mysteries and thrillers, he decided to give writing a try. Several novels later, he can honestly say he has found his calling. He is married and lives in a hundred-year-old house. He is the author of the Lee Callaway Series, the Echo Rose Series, the Martin Rhodes Series, and the Hyder Ali Series.

Made in United States
Cleveland, OH
31 July 2025